Dough Boy

Peter Marino

Holiday House / New York

For Courtney Reid, Nancy White, Ellie Parker, Nancy Seid,
Kathleen Herold, Aaron Broadwell, Tom Ecobelli, and
Bill Reiss for their thoughtful critiques of my work.

Copyright © 2005 by Peter Marino
All Rights Reserved
Printed in the United States of America
www.holidayhouse.com

First Edition

1   3   5   7   9   10   8   6   4   2

Library of Congress Cataloging-in-Publication Data
Marino, Peter, 1960–
Dough Boy / by Peter Marino.— 1st ed.
p. cm.
Summary: Overweight fifteen-year-old Tristan, who lives happily with his divorced mother
and her boyfriend, Frank, suddenly finds that he must deal with intensified
criticism about his weight and other aspects of his life when Frank's popular
but troubled, nutrition-obsessed daughter moves in.
ISBN 0-8234-1873-1 (hardcover)
[1. Weight control—Fiction. 2. Family problems—Fiction. 3. Divorce—Fiction.
4. Teasing—Fiction. 5. Bullies—Fiction. 6. Friendship—Fiction. 7. High schools—Fiction.
8. Schools—Fiction.] I. Title.
PZ7.M338782Do 2005
[Fic]—dc22
2004040593

ISBN-13: 978-0-8234-1873-2
ISBN-10: 0-8234-1873-1

Chapter 1

My parents were college professors and not too well acquainted with a kitchen, so to them a hot lunch only meant something that had been left out in the sun. Because of that, when I was younger, I'd loved lunch at school. A hot meal in the middle of the day, no food poisoning. The food had not been very good, but meeting up with other captives, eating junk, and playing afterward excited me.

By high school my enjoyment of school lunches had dwindled. Something was at work, a self-consciousness about eating in front of people. Partly this was because of our school's diet fads. By the time I was in ninth grade, I ate quickly and never had anything chocolaty or fattening on my tray, for fear of violating some nutritional ordinance.

The worst fad was called extreme eating. You stuck to vegetables and low-cal dressings, skim milk, diet sodas. All the athletes, male and female, were doing it, the cheerleaders, too, of course. Even some of my not-so-athletic and/or popular friends were eating extremely. While having lunch with my friend Peter, I noticed that he had brought a huge Tupperware bowl of lettuce to school.

"What're you doing, Pete?"

"Lunch. You need to try this. I lost five pounds."

"No dressing?" I asked.

"Oh yeah." He jumped up and came back with little paper packets of salt and pepper, which he sprinkled onto the lettuce. Then he began to eat.

"You're skinny," I said. "You don't weigh much more than five pounds."

"Flab. My dad told me if I don't get rid of it now, I'll have a big beer gut like him when I get older. He's trying it, too."

Why would Peter want an even skinnier body than he had? And who was he trying to impress? His interactions with most humans outside of school were by way of a computer monitor. As for his father, he didn't just have a beer gut going—it was more of a Henry VIII look. I knew a Henry VIII look well because of my interest in English history. (Unlike extreme eating, this was not a hobby that promoted popularity.)

But maybe there *was* something to Peter's diet plan—he wanted to stay thin so he wouldn't grow up to look like his old man. So would the reverse of that reasoning work for me? If I stayed fat now, would I grow up to look like my thin old man? People have hoped for dumber things.

My best friend, Marco Cavi, also participated, but that was all for show. He would stick to a very strict low-carbohydrate diet when people were watching him, talk the talk, making up facts and statistics, something he was good at. But home was another story. The Cavis' refrigerator looked like an airplane hangar, and it was always full. I never had the nerve to call Marco on eating watercress at school and then deep-fried potato croquettes at home, but what was the use? No matter what he ate, he was in great shape.

Fortunately the extreme eating craze died before tenth grade. Still there were little eating vogues that came and went, month by month. Our cafeteria may have provoked these fads because it was pretty clear the nutritionists had flunked out of college. Rumor had it the food was all government surplus, although no one knew which government. Come to think of it, the names of the dishes made you wonder if it was actually food they were dredging up. Pot Pie Pipers and Cheddar Surprise Blank Casserole and Mock Pizza Curls. The hot meals were not easy to identify. You wouldn't look and say, "Oh, that's ziti," or "That must be hamburger casserole." Instead you'd have to describe it, for example, "Oh, those are tadpole-shaped chunks floating in a sauce that looks like melted crayons."

Yet every day our principal, Mr. Matthews, would nasally announce the lunch menu as if he were not repulsed by it: *"Today is C Day. Please follow your schedule for C Day. Today's menu includes, and please listen carefully, Chicken Nibbles, fluffed rice, carrots glazed with ketchup, half-pint milk, and cookie. Please take only two napkins per person."* Occasionally he even treated us to his zany sense of humor: *"And remember, don't eat the napkins. Haw haw."*

But the food issue obviously bored Mr. Matthews. The one thing he really and truly believed to be depraved was students parking their cars diagonally. He would deliver long, passionate lectures about responsible parking and how the yellow lines were painted for a reason. Then, as if sensing that his unseen audience had tuned him out, he'd bark into the microphone: *"Do not park beyond the yella lines!"* Presumably he then went back to his office and punched a wall before slipping back into his coma.

However, even Mr. Matthews could not do anything about Will Zumigata's surviving birth or his continued existence. Will was one of my self-consciousness boosters. The first time I can remember his haunting me was when I was in sixth grade, during my first week in middle school. He saw me standing near my locker with my hands closed on my hips.

"What are you, a girl," he said. It wasn't a question. When I didn't say anything, he said, "You've got your hands on your hips like a girl. Who do you think you are, Lady Lard?" For three days I was afraid I would have a new nickname, and, as you know, a nickname in school can stick with you forever.

Anyway, Will taught me that a boy, fat or thin, keeps his hands open if he's got them on his hips. He was a senior and teased me like I was a kid brother. However, kid brothers often hate and want to murder the older brothers who tease them. Sometimes he would wrap his arm playfully around my neck and want to know how the Dough Boy was doing, poking me in the stomach. "Come on, Dough Boy, giggle." Then he'd let me go as if the whole thing were a brotherly ritual we did.

Will Zumigata's kindly observations about my body were the only real constant from middle school to high school. My home life had changed dramatically since my parents were now divorced and with other people. Extreme eating would turn out to be nothing compared to the delights life had in store for me in tenth grade, inside and outside of school.

Chapter 2

If I felt like pitying myself, I could blame my parents and claim that none of my tenth-grade disasters would have happened if they had stayed married. But if most kids have a hard time with divorce, I was an exception—it was the right thing for them to do. Mom and Dad were great about it; I had as solid a relationship with them as a boy from a "broken" home could have. They both had a wicked sense of humor—my mother especially—and I was proud to have inherited it. And I had never been under the delusion that their marriage was meant to last forever; there was a sinister double meaning to the wedding vow "until death do us part."

In my early days, long before they lovingly planned their divorce, Mom and Dad fought often. But after the storm was over, they would laugh at how badly they had behaved—that was how they made up. However, by eighth grade, their fights were flourishing, and the comical makeup sessions happened less and less. One Saturday afternoon they were in the kitchen battling over something that neither of them can remember now. I was in the living room on the couch like a loaf. At one point Dad was yelling hard at Mom who was screaming back, "Louder, Gordon, louder. See if you can break a few more blood vessels." Dad stopped yelling. Then I heard him laugh, like he was very tired.

"We need to break up, don't we?" he said.

Mom, calm now, too, responded, "I guess we do."

"I think we need to spare our little boy all this craziness," he said.

I turned on the TV to some numbskull show so I couldn't hear what they were saying. Then they came into the living room, red faced and tousled, hand in hand.

"Tristan," Mom said. "Tri, we have something to tell you." I clicked off the TV and sat up to face them.

"You know how much we love you," Dad said.

"And this doesn't have anything to do with me," I said.

"Right," said Mom.

"And you just want me to be happy," I said.

"Right," said Dad.

"And you're getting divorced," I said.

"Right," they both answered.

"Well, I'm happy if you're happy. Are you happy?"

"Yes," said Mom. "Very, very happy."

"I think it's the right thing, son," Dad said.

"But are you happy, Dad? That's what I asked."

"Yes, I'm happy."

"All right then. We're all happy. Let's get divorced."

They both gave me foolish, patronizing smiles.

"Why, it's as if you knew this was coming," Dad said.

It wasn't really all sweet and happy, as you could probably guess. When Mom and I helped Dad move into his condo just outside our village, Green Hills, Mom began to cry. Suddenly pain, real pain, propelled through my entire body. Something was changing forever. Absolute loss. Dad would only be a few minutes away by car, so it wasn't like the arrangements some kids had, seeing their fathers every other weekend, maybe less. But he would never again live with me and Mom together. I would never have that back.

I was supposed to be devastated by the divorce, and I was supposed to join Banana Splits at school and give voice to my rage by drawing pictures of my house broken in two. But the fact was, my parents would be happier apart. They would still see each other since they were both anthropology professors at the state university. Maybe working in the same place and being married had been too much togetherness. Maybe that's why they were always at each other's throats. Or maybe they just didn't get along.

I had three friends who I'd been in band with since sixth grade, Peter, Anthony, and Gretchen. All three of them had divorced parents. Peter's mother had dumped his father and moved in with another guy, but Peter and his brothers didn't even seem to notice. They just continued playing video games and pounding one another. Gretchen couldn't understand why her mother hadn't left her father a long time before she did. "He could drive someone nuts," she said matter-of-factly. "Besides, my parents had a commuter marriage. Now they can just stay home—alone."

Anthony's parents had never officially gotten married, so maybe he had no right to claim he was in the same club as us when they split. Yet Anthony was the only one who complained. He blamed his mother for the breakup, even though his father had taken off on them. Then he shifted the blame to his stepfather, hating the guy for taking his father's place. His stepfather was a science teacher in the middle school, and after he married Anthony's mother, he aged ten years in a month—living in a house with a kid who hates you can do that to a person. They divorced eventually, and Anthony hated his stepfather for leaving his mother. Anthony had some problems with logic.

I did have a few worries about my parents' splitting. Would my father start a new family? Would I end up with an evil stepmother? I was more worried that my mother would marry someone who was a real jerk and then I would have to spit out the word *stepfather* like Anthony did.

Dad quickly got involved with a woman named Cyndi who was a lot younger than him. She looked nineteen, but she turned out to be twenty-nine, with a high, squeaky, little-girlish voice. I tried to whip up a little resentment on the possibility that she and Dad had been seeing each other all along, that she was the cause of the breakup. But I couldn't get a good grip on that resentment because Cyndi was likeable in many ways. She had a different kind of humor than

Mom and Dad. She was ironic and self-deprecating but very quietly so. That, along with the fact that she was really cute, made her easy to get along with.

She was also somewhat round, which looked good on her, though she didn't think so. Cyndi could appreciate the complications of fatness. She would wink at me when we were enjoying a dinner that contained enough calories for several nutrition pyramids. That wink said, "Eat, drink, and be merry, for tomorrow I start another failed diet." From what I observed of her, she didn't eat like she was storing up for a hard winter—she just had one of those bodies that couldn't throw anything away.

Mom also got a quick start on the dating scene, so quick that I teased her that the real reason her marriage had broken up was that Dad wouldn't allow her to date other guys. At first she complained about "all the losers out there," making it sound as if there was a vast, secret society of desperate men who came out at night to drive single women insane. "I just can't seem to find a guy worth fighting with like your father," she sighed.

Finally she met Frank, who, like me, was a person of bulk. I could tell from the start that he was a keeper. They just clicked together, got along like Mom never had with Dad. Well, she did try to screw it up, although I don't think she knew she was trying to. Where Mom was high-strung and argumentative, Frank was very even tempered. But he would get sullen and pouty over even a suspicion of harshness from her and she had to learn some patience around him.

I liked Frank. Like Cyndi, he loved to eat. Unlike Cyndi, he often warned me of the dangers of dieting. He would recite a short speech about how a person simply needed to eat right and exercise. Then he would burst out laughing because it was no secret that Frank's definition of eating right meant eating right away. And exercise meant taking an aerobic nap after dinner. I began to wonder if Cyndi and Frank weren't my real parents.

Frank was black, tall, and broad shouldered, and handsome in a studious way. There was a slight sadness about him that I sensed but could not describe. Then again old people my parents' age always looked sad or tired. Anyway, Frank had cultivated a perfectly round stomach over the years. One night he fixed the three of us small bowls of ice cream, dressed properly with hot fudge, a sprinkle of nuts, and a cap of whipped cream. We all sat in front of the TV in the family room of his house eating them, me in a semi-hypnotic state. As I dug my way near the bottom of the bowl, I felt my mother's eyes on me. I gave her a friendly sneer, then finished what was left, licking my spoon purposefully.

"It's a small bowl, Mom."

She smiled. "I was just thinking that there's love in this room."

Frank looked up with that drunken face babies have after they've been nursed.

"Huh?"

"You two look so happy," she said.

Frank scraped the bowl with his spoon. "I hope there's no insinuation there, woman," he said.

"You're both so defensive. No one is ever going to know you're not related."

Frank looked at me, raised his bowl as if for a toast. "Here's to the woman from Planet Thin," he said. I clinked my bowl to his.

I definitely liked Frank.

By the summer between ninth and tenth grade, Mom and Frank made Frank's place the nest, which was fine with me. He was a photographer with his own commercial studio and had a beautiful house outside of town that overlooked a woods with an enormous barn for the horses he used to have before his divorce. They were his daughter's horses, so I guess there were too many memories to keep them around. He gave me a huge room compared to mine at home, and it had its own bathroom.

The best part was Dad moved back into our house when Mom moved out, so I didn't have to give up my childhood home. And it also meant that even though Frank's house was in a different district, I didn't have to switch schools. Mom and Dad finally laughed together again, this time about how cozy everything had become. "That's what was missing from our marriage," Mom said. "Frank and Cyndi."

I spent one week with Dad and one with Mom, but neither of them had a fit when I had to make other arrangements to accommodate my schedule. Cyndi and Frank were easy about it, too. All told, we got along fine.

That is, we got along fine until Frank's daughter, Kelly, sharpened her teeth and decided to come back. Pictures of her indicated that her mother was most likely white. Kelly had been on shaky terms with Frank since he and her mother had gotten an ugly divorce a few years before. She was sixteen now, a junior at a high school near Buffalo. Frank, being the quiet sort of guy he was, hadn't said much about her, and I hadn't pressed him.

One day Kelly called Frank unexpectedly and asked to have dinner with him, so he drove to Buffalo to meet her. This might seem like a good, healthy direction for their relationship, but for me it was the beginning of an out-of-control sleigh ride.

After Kelly and Frank had their reconciliation dinner, she came to stay for a weekend. I offered to hide out at my father's while this was going on, but Frank said no.

"You're part of the family now," he said. "Besides, if your mother and I ever get married—" He and Mom looked away from each other as if they needed to spit something into a napkin. "I mean, if we ever, you know, make things more permanent, then she should get to know both of you now."

"That's fine, Frank," I said. "I'd like to meet her."

"Uh, Tristan, um . . ." Frank said.

"Yeah?"

"There's, uh, something I need to tell you about Kelly."

"Okay. Shoot."

"Well, I love her and all."

"You're her father."

"Well, what I mean is, to put it mildly, Kelly's . . . difficult."

"Difficult? Like she's into explosives difficult?"

"Oh, I might as well say it," he said, putting a hand on my shoulder. "Tristan, Kelly is planning to be . . ." He looked away.

"Go on," I said.

He blurted, "She's going to be a nutritionist."

A tiny breath sucked into my lungs.

"I know, I know," he said. "She's a real athletic girl. Health conscious. Preachy. Do you know the type?"

"Like the school nurse when I get weighed for my physical?"

"Yes. I'm only telling you this so you'll be prepared. She rails against anything that keeps people from being bone-thin, like a sandwich. Be careful of traps. That's basically what I have to tell you."

"Do you mean she's anorexic?"

"Oh no," he said. "No, Kelly is an expert on healthy eating and exercise. She has a hearty appetite, but for things that are *good* for you, you know? She prefers—let's say—a leaner look." He cleared his throat as if to cough out the euphemism.

"Are you trying to tell me she actually eats five servings of fruits and vegetables a day?"

"Yes."

"That's just not right, Frank."

"I know. To think any daughter of mine . . ."

"Are you sure I shouldn't stay at my dad's when she comes?"

"Oh no," my mother burst in. "You're not abandoning me in my hour of need. You're staying."

"Well, what do *you* have to worry about?" I asked her. "I'm the one who's gonna be getting the lectures."

"That's not all," Frank said. "It's not just the nutrition thing."

"What could be worse than that?" I asked. "What could possibly be worse than that?"

"She's . . . difficult. In general. About lots of things."

"And you're not leaving me," Mom said. "Forget about it."

"Okay, okay."

"Be careful of traps," Frank said. "I don't know how else to put it."

"I'm already trapped," I said, "unless I can lose fifty pounds by the weekend."

"Be careful of traps, my boy," Frank said again, almost absently, and walked away.

I went to my room and sat on the bed for a while, worrying. A nutrition-major type. She would descend on me like a vulture. Eventually my fear was balanced by a curiosity about Kelly. Throughout the house, there were pictures of her at different ages. She'd started out as a chubby girl, then gotten skinnier as she grew up. She was always very pretty, and as she got older, she became stunningly beautiful. And she had a body that could win a few medals. Kelly had enormous brown eyes with a faintly mischievous twinkle in them. She wasn't the kind of girl I would ask out, since I never asked anybody out. Unlike me, Kelly had never lacked for dates, I was sure.

I considered fasting. I considered jogging for forty-eight hours straight. There was always do-it-yourself liposuction or wearing a rubber suit until I sweated it off. But mainly I was curious, very curious about Kelly, and just a little excited.

Chapter 3

When I met Kelly, I immediately forgot about Frank's warning because she was so gorgeous I was embarrassed to be alive. She had the confidence of someone considerably older. I wanted her approval. I wanted her to be happy with the new family arrangement. I wanted her to marry me.

And Kelly was happy with the new family arrangement, for the better part of an entire hour. She charmed the pants off all of us during those first fifty-nine minutes. She was talkative and funny, taking a fervent interest in Mom and me. Frank was practically glowing.

Then we sat down to dinner.

"Let's say grace," she said, putting her hands out. Fearing my palms would be clammy, I shyly took her hand. Closing her eyes, Kelly began the invocation. "Bless us, O Lord, and these thy gifts, which are about to receive from thy plentiful bounty, through Christ, our Lord." That sounded like an ending, so I started to pull my hand away, but Kelly held tight and continued speaking: "And,

Lord, let us eat to nourish our bodies with the food you have given us. Let us not eat to excess. In the spirit of healing, let us not eat more than we need or truly want." It sounded like she was finished this time, but Kelly was not done with us yet.

"And, Lord? Please forgive us all for our faults. And please forgive me for the resentments I harbor against others. Help me to learn to let go."

Yes, I thought, learn to let go of my hand.

She looked up, her gigantic, beautiful eyes sparkling. "Let's eat. I'm starved."

Mom and Frank had made a sort of vegetarian lasagne and bought multigrain bread from Spring House Bakery. Everything was almost entirely lacking in fat, and despite this shortcoming, it looked and tasted good. Though I knew I would pay in hunger later, I ate sparingly. Mom peppered Kelly with questions and I tried to follow her.

Kelly's patience didn't last long.

"So, Kelly," Mom said, "are you studying any foreign languages at school?"

"You ask so many questions," Kelly replied, as if she was admonishing a three-year-old. "I'm sure my father could have given you my profile before I came." She sighed, stabbed at some greens. "Yes, French."

The smile remained on Mom's face, frozen and idiotic now.

"You know, Anne, and actually this goes for you, too, Tristan," Kelly said, looking at me, "you don't have to worry about me. I know what you're thinking. 'Oh, she must be going through a lot of feelings right now being in her old house full of strangers. A lot of stuff must be coming up for her.' Well, you're right. I am processing a lot. But they are my feelings. You aren't really helping by trying to take my mind off things with idle conversation." Then she laughed. "That just interferes with my processing process."

I laughed too hard.

She looked at me with a condescending smile. "It wasn't that funny."

"Oh," I said, sucker punched. "Okay."

"Tristan's studying French and Latin," Frank said defiantly. "There's nothing idle about that." Actually I'd taken a half year of Latin in eighth grade and that was it.

"Good for him," Kelly said. She curled a lasagne noodle around her fork.

We choked down the rest of the meal in record time. Rather than eating it, Kelly pushed her food around her plate and murmured things like "carbohydrates" in irritated puffs. During the unusually efficient and soundless cleaning of the table, I whispered to Mom in the kitchen, "Should I go to Dad's tonight?"

"I stayed up all night with you when you had chicken pox."

"I was five months old."

"The least you could do is stand by me during this storm."

"But what if she starts on the F-A-T thing?" I said, a touch desperate.

"Then bring up the W-I-T-C-H thing," she said.

I glared at her a second, then went into the family room where Frank and Kelly sat watching a rerun of *The Beverly Hillbillies*. Frank sat on the couch while Kelly sat on a hard wooden chair across from him. There would be no ice cream served this evening.

"What's on?" I asked with truly asinine enthusiasm.

Kelly looked up at me. "Some people do nothing but watch TV," she said. "Couch potatoes. America is getting fat and lazy."

She had used the f-word. The air was poisoned

now. "Yeah?" I said, feeling as dumb as I had ever felt, and plopping down in the elephant chair.

Mom came in after loading the dishwasher and sat down next to Frank for another attempt at civility.

"What are we watching?" she asked with a subdued smile. Kelly got up, found the remote, and muted the TV.

"Don't you hate TV when people are supposed to be talking to one another? Television puts up a wall between people."

I nodded like I had a spring for a neck.

"Any objections?" she asked, waving the remote. "I would feel a lot more comfortable if we could talk instead of sitting here like zombies." She clicked the TV off. "Although I should take a long walk after that starchy meal." She looked at her father and said, without mercy, "We all should. That stuff practically turns to sugar in your mouth. God knows how much insulin my poor pancreas had to churn out."

"Do you have diabetes?" my mother asked, surprised.

"No," Kelly said curtly. "Old fat people who've let themselves go get that type of diabetes. Tristan, how do you feel about your stepfather getting out of shape and putting his health in jeopardy?"

It was as if she had just vacuum sealed the room and I couldn't breathe. The only thing I could squeak out was, "Um, he's not exactly my stepfather." Then, panicked that I had said the wrong thing, I added, "Yet." That was still the wrong thing. "I mean, I haven't thought about it." There was more silence.

"That wasn't necessary," Frank said to Kelly, not quite sure of his voice.

"Hmm," said Kelly, and breathed in deeply.

We sat in that horrifying stillness for what seemed like one entire rotation of the earth until the phone rang with the subtlety of a fire bell. There was a combination of "I'll get it," "Got it," and "Probably for me" coming from Mom, Frank, and me as we all jumped up for it. But Frank was the lucky one who escaped to the kitchen. Seeing as there was no residual conversation in the family room, we could hear him. "Hello? Oh, hello. Yes, yes, yes. No. No problem. I'm fine. Good, good. She's fine. Here, I'll let you talk to her. Kelly!"

"I'll take it in my room," she called to him, and then added with force, "My *old* room." She flounced out.

"It's her mother," Frank said, returning. "Her *thin* mother."

"Frank," I started, "I didn't mean—"

"Don't," he interrupted. "Don't apologize for anything. That's her tactic, divide and conquer. Just watch your back. She'll have us both on Slim-Fast by the end of the weekend if we're not careful."

I got up to go to my room.

"Don't leave us," Mom said. She had never sounded so helpless before.

"I feel a nightmare coming on," I said. "I want to get an early start."

"Two days of this, eh?" she asked Frank as I was walking out.

"Yep," he replied. "Two carefree, lazy days."

I'd thought I was safe, for the evening, anyway. But Kelly came into my room shortly after I had shut my door, even though by our rules a shut door indicated privacy. Kelly evidently didn't understand this sign or didn't care. She knocked, then strolled in as if it didn't matter if I was asleep or naked or scratching. Fortunately, I was lying—clothed—on my bed distractedly reading ahead in *David Copperfield*. This book was assigned in some attempt to tie English 10 with European studies, even though we were still doing Charlemagne in European studies. Coordination wasn't a strong suit at Green Hills High.

"Hi." She sat down on the edge of my bed. I held the book in my hands like it might try to get away. Dew formed on my forehead. My face radiated heat good and hot—it wasn't sexual excitement, but rather a terrified thrill that the queen was in my room. Feeling as limber as a double-wide trailer, I sat up and managed a phlegmy, "Hi."

"We need to talk, don't we?" she asked.

"I guess," I said, although I didn't know about what. I merely wanted to please her. Her perfume, sharp and sweet, permeated my room. She could steamroll over me, and I wouldn't try to stop her.

"It's hard. Being heavy, I mean. I was overweight once. It hurt a lot, the things people used to say to me."

The front wheel of the steamroller just caught the tips of my toes.

"Oh," I said.

"You know, it was my father's fault mostly. He encouraged me to eat because he couldn't control his own self. I kept begging him to work out more and to stop eating crap. But he wouldn't listen. Never has."

"Oh."

"The last thing I said to him before we left was, 'You can run, but you still have to take yourself with you.' And there's a lot more of himself these days than there was." She paused, then said with a disgusted laugh, "And he's not doing too much running either."

"Uh-huh."

"So now he's in a new relationship."

"Yeah, I guess so. With my mother," I said, no brain waves.

"Detach with love, that's what I have to do. I can't help it if he gives himself a heart attack from all that junk he eats." I thought back to the ice cream bond Frank and I shared.

"Cholesterol," she said. "It's like he's never heard the word before."

"Yeah. Uh-huh."

"This used to be my exercise room."

"Oh."

"Yes, and my father wanted me to put my exercise bike and my mats in the cellar!"

"Yeah, uh . . ."

"But why shouldn't I look out at this view when I'm riding, especially in the winter?" she snapped as if I had anything to do with it. "Who wants to sit on an exercise bike in a dingy cellar in the dead of winter?"

"I wouldn't want to—"

"Let's go for a walk, you and me," she interrupted. "We don't even have to talk if you don't want to. I just want to do something for you. You're young. There's still hope for you, you know. This is the time, Tristan."

"Uh-huh." I cleared my throat again. I was still sitting up, despite having no spine.

"My father could drop dead of a major coronary any day now. He's almost fifty. You don't want to be constantly staring your future in the face every time you look at him, do you?"

"Okay." With a vocabulary this big, I was never going to be promoted to eleventh grade.

"Let's go then."

As coordinated as a bagful of Jell-O, I got up off the bed and followed her out. I would follow her anywhere, by the sheer force of her personality and my sheer lack of one.

The walk was even more humbling than I could have dreamed. Kelly had a stride like a giant, and I had to pretend it took no effort to keep up with her. However, my internal organs weren't as cooperative as my good intentions and very, very soon I was heaving gulps of air and sweating. Kelly didn't slow down to compensate. Maybe I could make a run for my dad's and hide there until she gave up looking for me. But she'd be as fast as a lynx and overtake me in seconds.

We got home an hour after we'd left, the longest hour I had ever endured, and I experienced my first moment of genuine happiness all evening. It was just a moment, though, because then Kelly explained her long-term plan to me.

"We'll do this every night when I'm here," she said. "But when I'm not here, you need to do the walking on your own. Walking is the best exercise of all. It's the best for the heart, the easiest on the skeletal system, and the best for weight loss." I blushed again, if that were possible underneath my wet and scarlet cheeks. She wasn't going to actually call me fat. She would settle for insinuation.

That night as I lay in bed, sticky and smelling of rising dough, I tried to work out a game plan. How could I stay at my father's every time Kelly was in town? Maybe I could get seriously ill whenever she was in from Buffalo? Nothing deadly, of course, just something close to deadly. But how long would I be able to keep that charade going? I tossed and turned, knowing Kelly would continue my treatment plan tomorrow, monitoring my meals and aerobicizing me hard, and despite all that, being totally beautiful.

Chapter 4

When I woke up the next morning, my stomach was singing its demands. I almost made a beeline for the kitchen and my routine bowl of Cheerios, when I remembered the new circumstances of my life. There had to be some way to get to Dad's. I could wait until I got there to eat three meals, maybe all at once.

Trying not to look like I was sneaking, I came out of my room. Kelly was still sleeping. This gave me a chance to shovel in the cereal. At first all three of us tiptoed around, fearing that too much noise would wake the commandant. When it became evident that Kelly slept as if she was anesthetized, we all started going about our business, slowly and with trepidation at first, then with more confidence. It started to feel like the house had been liberated. As it turned out, Kelly slept until nearly one in the afternoon, by which time the trepidation had relaxed, stretched its legs.

I decided to escape to Marco's house. Marco wasn't even supposed to be going to the same school as me, since his house was in the Putnam School District. But, after they had terrorized the Putnam faculty, his parents had switched him to Green Hills in second grade, even though they had to pay tuition. I think my being there was part of their decision, too, a big convenience for Marco, his parents, and the teachers who wouldn't have to fight him to get his homework done, since he'd get me to do it.

So that first Saturday of the Kelly Experience, I went off to his house, to help him get ready for the quiz on *David Copperfield*. He had actually attempted to read the CliffNotes, but found them too complicated. Both books had been tossed on the floor next to some underwear. To his credit, he had gone that extra mile and spent twenty minutes laboring on the Internet trying to find an easier summary of the story; and by the time I arrived, he was getting ready to go out. His date, Heather Baird, was so cool and curvaceous and poison-mouthed that I was almost afraid Marco might not be a match for her. It was late September, the weather was fine, the leaves were starting to get beautiful, and a boat ride on Lake Eight was the perfect first date. Marco was not allowed to use the boat alone, so he was bringing Heather along for safety.

I made a mental note to follow Marco's lead and start talking more often—and stupidly—about girls. I knew I should go out on a date sometime before I turned thirty.

I was leafing through the novel aimlessly because Marco wasn't paying attention, feeling a little more bored and taken advantage of than usual. He was going out on a date, while I had to fight for his attention to do his work for him. And I'd jumped at the opportunity to come over, so I felt just a little ashamed.

Marco was staring into the mirror, working on Stage One of hair preparation, with a towel wrapped around his waist from his recent shower. I started explaining *David Copperfield* from the beginning again, but he kept interrupting me with things like, "So the father dies and that's what the whole book is about?"

"That's what the first few whole chapters are about. I haven't read the whole book yet, remember?"

"So what the hell's his problem? If my father died I wouldn't write a book about it." Then he added, "I mean, I'd be sad and all."

He took off his towel and threw it on the floor.

He deodorized under his arms, then pulled on a tight maroon T-shirt.

"It's fiction. He wasn't real. He didn't write it. Someone else did."

"Yeah. So what's this book about?"

"This kid David is born—"

"Dave."

"Yeah, Dave Copperfield."

"Mr. Rylant is unprofessional," Marco said to his reflection. "He changed the whole curriculum."

"Yeah, well, there goes Dr. Seuss."

Marco paused for a second as if the possibility that he had just been insulted was trying to wiggle its way through his blood-brain barrier. Then he was back to his mirror, standing with his bottom half naked, intently examining his complexion. I went on to explain Mr. Murdstone, the main antagonist. "Can you remember that word, Marc? *Antagonist.* Mr. Murdstone is the antagonist."

"Mr. Flintstone," he said.

"Right. So Mr. Murdstone marries David's mother and pretty much squeezes the life out of her, and he beats the kid and sends him away to boarding school."

Marco turned and looked at me, incredulous.

He was actually stirred by this information. "That's bullshit. Mr. Flintstone. Why didn't the kid tell his real father?"

Even wearing only a T-shirt Marco didn't look ridiculous. The universe, blind to justice, had also provided him with a mature appendage. This was a stark contrast to my own boyish pacifier, which, despite its smallness, was impossible to camouflage during gym showers.

"His real father died, remember? So he couldn't tell him anything." Marco shook his head. "Because he was dead," I said, to reinforce.

"What about the teachers at school? Why didn't he tell them Mr. Flintstone was beating him up?"

"They were too busy changing the curriculum," I said. Marco turned again to the mirror. "He didn't go to school. Didn't you read any of this?"

"My father thinks I'm dys-a-lexic," he said without a wink or smirk to indicate he understood irony.

"Or at least trying to be," I said.

"Huh?"

"Nothing. So David Copperfield has to sit in the parlor and do his lessons, and Mr. Murdstone and his evil sister torment him all day by making him do the same lessons over and over. . . ."

Marco was bored again. "Beat him up? I would have kicked the crap out of him." He was now fully invested in doing his hair, having pulled on a pair of jeans but not without first blow-drying his pubic mound and powdering his crotch carefully. I took note of this, assuming it meant he had plans with Heather he was not going to tell me about. That was typical of Marco. He was taking out one of the hottest, scariest girls in school, and he was planning for the best.

Marco carefully spread mousse or gel through his hair like a sculptor. I was unfamiliar with such products. The extent of my hair grooming was holding my head over a heat vent before going out in subzero weather. And I had never considered using a hair dryer on my private area, though of course I wouldn't need to, not ever having company down there. Besides, if I ever tried it, I'd become one of those freak stories where the kid winds up in the burn unit and none of the hospital staff can keep a straight face.

Marco toyed with a belt, to wear one or not

wear one, then decided against it. "Just write out the plotline or whatever for me. That's all I need to re-fresh my memory." There was no arguing with that reasoning. I had been dismissed. He was picking up Heather at her house in town. Marco was a year older than the sophomore class and had his license already. He had really been driving since he was thirteen, but now he was doing it legally.

Evidently Mr. Murdstone, if nothing else, had caught his attention. While I lay on my stomach flipping through pages and figuring out an honor-able way to make an exit, Marco brought the belt down on my rear.

"Ow, you imbecile!" I shouted, and jerked around. Marco was already staring at his reflection in the mirror as if nothing had happened.

"You got to work out more, pussy," he said, as if working out would make my skin resistant to being whipped with a belt. Then, bored with his little joke, he said, "Are you gonna write out the summary for me or not? I've got a date, dude. You can stay if you want or you can go. Let yourself out. Use the computer if you want. My parents are in Florida."

"Cape Cod, you said before," I reminded him, sitting up and pretending I wasn't in acute pain.

"Oh, right. Cape Cod. I hate saltwater taffy. Anyway, if they call, tell them . . . no, don't answer. Listen, don't screw this up like Montreal. Just don't answer the phone."

"Thanks," I said, though sarcasm was usually lost on him.

"Later." I said nothing as he left, smelling Marco's cologne, sitting on his bed with my butt aching, and wondering exactly at what age I was going to join the teenage race.

Marco blasted back into the room.

"I totally forgot. What about your stepsister? Is she a babe?"

"Oh, come on," I said.

"No really. Is she cute or what?"

"I don't know."

"You don't know? You're a red-boned American boy and you don't know if she's cute?"

"Do you mean red-blooded?"

"Red-boned."

"Red-blooded," I said.

"Bones are covered with blood, right? So they'd be red inside your body. Who's the doofus now?"

"But the expression is—"

"Whatever."

I stared at him a few seconds, trying to remember what we were talking about. "She's Frank's daughter," I said. "I'm not supposed to notice things like that."

"She's your *step*sister. It's totally legal."

"She's not my stepsister, but still . . ." There was no gain in arguing with Marco. "She's cute."

"Body?"

"I don't know."

"You better know."

"Yeah, okay, she is."

"Hot?"

"Yes."

"Then say it. Say 'my stepsister is hot.'"

"No."

"What's the matter? Are you afraid of her or something?"

"No."

"So why . . ." he started, then smiled. "Never mind. I'll find out."

"What?"

"I don't remember her from Putnam."

"You left when you were in second grade. She looked different then."

"She's black, right?"

"What difference does that make?"

"Don't get girly on me. I wasn't saying anything. You're the one with the problem."

"Kelly's mother is white. Frank's black, like I told you before."

"Hot?"

"Yeah, Marco. Black, white, and hot."

"Cool. I'll check her out. See ya."

He was out the door again before I could start worrying about what a disaster it would be if I had to deal with Marco and Kelly in the same room. Heather Baird was practically an old notch in his bedpost already.

Marco Cavi and I had a weird relationship. Our parents had been friends at one time, but something had happened to make Mom and Dad cynical about the Fiero/Cavi family. His mother was a therapist, who for some reason my own mother now actively disliked. I don't know if Mom had once gone to her for counseling and something had gone terribly wrong or what. But she would always make insinuating remarks about Ms. Fiero, Master of Social Work (she, like Mom, had kept her family name) and how she reduced everything to feelings. "What feeling does that bring up?" Mom would say, mocking. "What event from your childhood does that remind you of?"

Marco's father—Dr. Cavi—was a plastic surgeon. Mom was convinced that Marco's parents were a professional team, getting patients in touch with their feelings enough to realize they needed nose jobs.

My mom and dad were a lot more conservative. For instance, they were old-fashioned in thinking that parents should actually set rules and raise the kid they brought into the world. Marco's life was not a model of perfection, but it was no small thrill being his friend considering his ease with everything around him, his free-flowing money, the lack of interference by his parents, and all the big, expensive toys he had.

He and I had been inseparable as kids. We used to hang out in his cellar, which was the size of anybody else's whole house, and we'd listen to music, play video games, watch TV, and eat his mother's delicious food. His father had built a dock so we spent hours swimming and playing in rubber rafts on Lake Eight. Marco's family tried to buy him some kind of diagnosis at school because of his bad grades, but he was just lazy. I would always help him with his homework—okay, do it for him, because the faster I got his work done, the more time we had to play. We had both been husky, but Marco made friends easily, picked fights, and made up just as easily, and generally barreled through life getting what he wanted as if that was the natural way of the world. He thought nothing of hauling off and slapping another kid when he was riled, and many times he provoked fights with me for the thrill of watching me go crazy with frustration. I was no match for him physically.

Sometimes, just for pure meanness, he would tease me until tears were squirting from my eyes. And sometimes he would try to start a fight just to see if I had gotten any scrappier since the last time.

Still, when he wasn't being a brat, he knew how to have a good time. Marco and I used to rummage through his attic like explorers, going through mysterious trunks and closets, crawling through the passageways between the finished attic walls and the inside surface of the roof. When we got a little older, he took me out on the family boat that he was not supposed to take out alone. He could always get someone to drive us somewhere whenever we needed. When his parents were home, they always insisted on taking us to dinner, treating us to ice cream, buying us drive-through food.

Then, something awful happened: Marco went through puberty and I didn't. Well, I did start, but my pituitary gland was a slow learner. I remember being excited that I was sprouting underarm hair by sixth grade and a couple pubies down below, too. But the celebration was premature because by the time ninth grade was finished I was still getting there, a few new developments every year but no sign of completion. I always had a babyish, flabby look, and worse, my voice refused to change. Now, at fifteen, I was still mistaken for a girl on the phone, although my parents—and their partners—were convinced they could hear it getting deeper by the day.

Marco, on the other hand, had sailed through puberty like a Polaroid developing. Besides all the necessary hair growing in thick and fast, his voice dropped quickly. And, most discouraging of all, by now he had lost all traces of baby fat and grown tall and lean. All of a sudden he had muscles and long, manlike legs. Mine looked like raw turkey drumsticks.

With Marco having the physique of an athlete and my staying a giant toddler, you'd think we'd fall away from each other when we became teenagers, and it was happening, slowly and steadily. I didn't want to think about it. We kept hanging around together, just not as much. Marco had girls in his life now, which meant less social time for me, although it also meant he had less time and tolerance than ever for schoolwork. Teachers continued to make unreasonable demands on him, which made my role as his tutor more urgent. But I'm not sure why I stuck around.

Part of it was that Marco was now very popular at school, and somehow that gave me recognition, like a backup singer. He never appeared to be embarrassed about being friends with me, no matter how nondescript I was. I was always at his parties, which hordes of kids came to. So I kept coming, often feeling like I had gotten too old for my role in his life, and like I was hanging around with someone who was turning into a stranger.

Marco's allusion to Montreal was probably another reason I was so obedient to him. He and I had joined the International Friendship Club at school in ninth grade, right at the beginning of the year, to get to know some of the cool kids. The club was packed, meeting in the cafeteria at night, and right away there was a trip to Montreal. I wrote both my and Marco's essays about why we should be included in the trip, and we got to go. We met the bus at the high school before daybreak one Saturday morning, and we were in our hotel room in Montreal by ten o'clock.

I liked what I saw of Montreal, but the trip wasn't just about sight-seeing. Marco had quickly ingratiated us in with the older guys, even Will Zumigata who was the coolest upperclassman. Will had set his sights on making fun of a strange sophomore named Wayne Funke, shouting lyrics to a retro acid rock song into his face whenever he had the chance. Everyone laughed, even me, though I was forcing it out. Maybe Will wouldn't remember me next. Pretty soon Marco had gotten us invited to Will's room Saturday night for the absolute hottest, by-invitation-only party in the hotel. I held on to a beer can all night, pouring the contents down the bathroom sink when I thought no one was looking. I tried to drink some, but by the third gulp I was holding my breath like I was swallowing goldfish.

Marco had different tastes. He drank the beer as if he liked it, and pretty soon he might as well have been a senior for the way he worked the room. We left the party at about twelve, Marco entrusting me to walk directly behind him in the hallway to our room to make sure he didn't sway or stagger if we ran into the authorities. Once we were safely back, Marco had almost immediately barfed into a wastepaper can. For the next hour or so he held his head over it and cried and whimpered and gagged so hard I was sure a lung had collapsed.

"Should I go get somebody?" I asked him.

"No-ho-ho," he cried, and gave over to more wracking.

There was a knock on the door, which invigorated Marco to grab the can and run into the bathroom. Mr. Leonard, one of the IFC advisers and also one of the youngest teachers in school, was standing there. Mr. Leonard always talked in this forced, formal tone, as if he was afraid people wouldn't take him seriously because he was so young.

"We're looking for Wayne Funke," he said, no hint of suspicion. "Is he here? Have you seen him?"

"No," I said.

"His roommate said he went out and hasn't come back."

Then I blurted out the dumbest thing I could have blurted out: "No, no one's here except me and Marco. He's really sick."

Mr. Leonard's head jerked up. "What?"

"Uh, he doesn't feel well."

He assumed an even more authoritarian tone. "Where is he?"

"In bed."

Mr. Leonard flipped on the lights and there was Marco's bed, still made, unoccupied.

"Any other suggestions, Tristan?"

"Um . . ."

Mr. Leonard tried the bathroom door. It was open. Marco lay slumped over the bathtub, which was puddled with vomit. The room stunk like it was trying to discourage predators.

"I see. Very sick indeed, Mr. Cavi. How much have you had to drink?"

"Nothing," he muttered, then let loose a particularly disgusting retch.

"Indeed."

Mr. Leonard stayed a miserably long time, making sure Marco was not going to need ambulance service, and helping me get him into bed.

"Some people will never go on another trip," he said as he was leaving the room.

The next day word got around, not so much that Marco had puked himself nearly dead, but that I had opened my big mouth.

"Dough Boy," Will Zumigata said in front of everyone, "why did you open your little boy mouth?"

It was a reasonable question, but not one I could answer.

"Someone needs to roll you into the oven."

It was Marco who ultimately saved me, who came to my defense, because I was like a servant or a dog he had to protect. He was persuasive enough to sway the hostility from me to Mr. Leonard, who might as well have been Satan by the time Marco got done with him. And while I had to tread lightly around Marco and all his new friends on that prolonged bus ride home on Sunday, by the time we got back to Green Hills, I seemed to have been forgiven, and as usual, forgotten. Just for good measure, Will grabbed my fat sides from behind as I was getting off the bus and gave them a hellish, playful jiggle.

For some reason, Mr. Leonard did not contact our parents, and he didn't report us to the vice principal either. He was right that some people would never go on another trip, because I was too scared to go back to IFC when we got home. Marco wasn't.

So "Montreal" was code between us. Whenever

I came close to displeasing Marco, he would mention Montreal and I'd come back to my senses.

But this wasn't the same as letting him copy my lab write-ups or doing his Course II math homework. This was going into my home—one of them—and taking on someone we were all afraid of. I was curious as to how such a meeting of the strong willed would turn out, but mainly I was hoping he would forget about Kelly the same way he did our English assignments.

Chapter 5

I walked back home. Kelly had arisen and my mother was tense. Frank was nowhere in sight, and judging from her formfitting leotard, Kelly was getting ready to exercise.

"Tristan," she said, "you have five seconds to decide if you want to come to exercise class with me. I'm late."

"Tristan needs to spend some time with his old mother," Mom said. Kelly breezed out the door and a few seconds later Frank's car started in the garage.

"Frank here?" I asked.

"He's in the barn."

"Doing what?"

"Feeding the horses."

"The horses that are gone now?"

"All right then, he's sulking, if you must know."

"What happened?"

"She told him he was the size of a truck."

"We knew that was coming."

"But the look on his face, Tri. It was like this: He's trying to interact with her, get onto some subjects they both like, and soon they're getting along fine. They both liked the horses, they both like the woods. They used to hike together. They get laughing even. Then, when she's got him trusting her, she lays this on him. That look on his poor face."

"So she actually said he was the size of a truck? What did she compare me to? A minivan?"

"No. She knew better than to criticize you in front of me."

"So what happened next?"

"She was trying to be tactful. 'I'm so worried. You've gotten so big.' And Frank is muttering things like 'I try to walk.' Then she just blurts out: 'You're the size of a truck. You can't let yourself go like that.'"

"And he—"

"He tried to steer her off the subject."

"And she wouldn't have it."

"Not a bit. She was looking for a fight and she got it."

"I'd better go to Dad's."

"If you go to Dad's, I can't stay," she said sadly. "No, it's you and me against the world."

Frank dragged himself away from his solitude to have a pleasant dinner with us, pleasant meaning

Kelly didn't pursue her truck theme. Later I fell asleep reading on my bed and woke up after a short time with my stomach rumbling. But it was impossible to grab a snack while Kelly was around. Before I had even focused, she was standing in my room, again without knocking.

"Time for our walk," she said. "I promised. I always keep a promise." She looked toward the door. "Unlike other people."

Whenever I'm walking or riding my bike, I seem to be a target for people in vehicles. Someone's just got to shout an insult at the fat kid. Here I am finally getting some exercise and these faceless people shout at me. There's no way to prevent it, and there's no getting revenge. At least so I thought until I met Kelly.

While we were at an intersection just outside of town, a truck pulled up to the stop sign.

"Keep working it off, fat boy. You need the exercise," a gravelly voice yelled from the cab. He then took off.

Kelly bent over, wound up like a pitcher, and threw something at the truck. There was a solid clang. The truck screeched to a dead stop.

"This is our turn." Kelly grabbed my shirt and

ran me into the woods. I sprinted like I knew how, and we came out behind a convenience store. She pushed me into the men's room.

"I'll call Dad," she said. She pulled the door closed.

I locked the door and waited for someone to pound on it, the fat basher in the truck, the police, the store manager. But no one did. Maybe fifteen minutes went by, a long time when you're standing in a convenience store bathroom with not much to do. There was a soft knock. I hesitated, then I heard Kelly's voice. "Tristan, it's me. Come on."

I opened the door. "Hurry up. Dad's waiting." She gave me a slight push in the direction of the front of the store where Frank was.

"Take us home, Dad," Kelly said.

"What happened?" he asked.

"Some piece of trash wouldn't leave us alone. He kept stopping."

Frank tried to push her for details.

"I don't want to talk about it," she said, loud and forceful. "I know when someone's dangerous. Let's go home."

"Well shouldn't I at least let the police know there's someone dangerous harassing children?"

"Children," she said, disgusted. "Forget about it. Drive, will you?"

Frank gave up. He probably did that a lot with her.

Kelly, sitting in the front seat with Frank, looked straight ahead the whole time. As we got close to home, she turned to me.

"We had a walk and a run tonight, Tristan," she said. "If we get chased every night, you'll be down to your natural weight in no time."

Frank let out a soft groan. But the judgment passed through me without a sting. Kelly had slapped back at the truck shouter for me. I still wanted her to go back to Buffalo, but she was obviously a person you wanted on your side.

Chapter 6

Two weekends later I was back at Mom's.

"Where's Frank?" I asked when I came into the house.

"Picking Kelly up at the train station," she said, looking away from me like a coward.

"Mom, look me in the eye."

She turned around, shrugged her shoulders. "It's his house. His kid. She had such a wonderful weekend last time she wanted to try it again."

"So why not last weekend when I was gone?"

"I can't dictate these things, Tri."

The next day I barely saw Kelly since she slept late again. I called Marco and tried to get myself invited over, but he had other plans.

"So, when is Kelly coming back?"

"How'd you know her name?"

"I never forget a name," he said, even though he had forgotten the names of every U.S. president, including the current one.

"Yes, you do. You forget stuff all the time."

"Not when a girl's involved. So when's she coming back?"

I couldn't lie quickly enough, so I hesitated.

"Is she there now?" He was excited.

"She's still asleep," I said, like I had just betrayed the whereabouts of the jewel safe.

"Don't bother to come by here," he said. "I'll be seeing you later today." He didn't elaborate, but it was definitely a warning. Late in the afternoon I lay down on my bed to read for a while. When I got bored with that, I opened my door and heard voices in the family room. Marco had infiltrated the premises and was talking in his smoothest tones. I snuck into the bathroom to gargle and make sure my hair wasn't too hilarious, then walked in on the gathering, faking not being a bit nervous. Marco was in the elephant chair and Kelly was on the couch. I had interrupted something.

"Dude," Marco offered. "Your mother invited me to dinner."

"You didn't tell me about Marco," Kelly said. She sounded pleased for real. "You've got some nice friends. Finally, someone I can talk to."

"Where's everybody?" I asked.

"Oh, I got rid of them. They were acting like Marco and I were deaf and needed an interpreter. Your mother's making something. I hope that's not meat I smell cooking. I should have told her beforehand what I can eat."

"Yeah," said Marco. "I'm doing low fat, too. Proteins."

"Meat's a protein, Marco," I said.

"So, you run?" she asked him, turning slightly from me.

"I used to do indoor track in the winter. And track and football, but I've got this Achilles tendon."

Liar. Marco could run like a panther. And I was tempted to ask him how to spell *Achilles*.

"I do field hockey, basketball, and track in the spring," she said, like she was listing household chores. "I got in trouble with field hockey for taking two weekends off to come here. I'm dumping basketball for a total body-conditioning thing they're doing at my school now. Basketball is too much time. Too much politics."

"Yeah!" Marco said as if he'd finally figured out what *x* stood for in the equation. "That's why I never tried out for basketball. Bus trips all the time. My parents said no. It would affect my grades."

Marco did so try out for basketball, in seventh and eighth grades. He got cut the first round of try-outs both years, even though his parents had promised the coach they would hire someone to work with him until his game improved. By ninth grade he was too prideful to subject himself to that kind of humiliation again.

"It's just listening to the girls all the way there and back and then homework when you get home so late," said Kelly.

"Totally. I hate doing homework at ten at night, and then you have to go to bed and get up and it starts all over."

I was trying to figure out what started all over for Marco when I realized they had forgotten I was in the room. That is, until Kelly punched the air out of me yet again by asking in a way that sounded only half joking, "Tristan, don't you have any manners, boy? Get your friend something to drink. What do you want to drink, Marco?"

Marco wanted soda, I'm sure, but that would betray his preference for white sugar, and he was temporarily above such a nutritional sin. "Uh, just water. Got any spring water?"

"Spring water. I'll check," I said.

"I'll have a Diet Coke," Kelly said. "Lemon, please."

I nodded automatically and went to the kitchen to get drinks and maybe a fire extinguisher for my face. Frank was deeply involved in examining various vegetables and fruits, trying to throw a meal together that would satisfy Kelly and not disgust the rest of us.

"How's it going?" Mom asked.

"Great. I told Kelly you were making a roast beef. Rare."

"What?" Frank asked.

"Yeah, she wanted to know why you didn't have any organ meat."

Mom got it and smiled. "Well, we could serve calf brains. That would be the first brain in Marco's body."

Frank was trying to separate bad leaves of lettuce from those that might be resurrected. "You joke around, Tristan, but it's my life flashing before my eyes here."

"Yeah? What's this about inviting Marco for dinner, Ma? Wasn't Mr. Murdstone free?"

She looked at me, puzzled. "I didn't invite him. Kelly did. And who's Mr. Murdstone?"

"Kelly just sent me in here to get drinks for them," I said, trying to emphasize the injustice. "*Sent* me."

Frank shook his head. "I'm trying not to think," he said. "Don't make me think right now."

Mom got the water for Marco, which was straight from the spring that fed our kitchen sink, and she poured some generic diet cola for Kelly, which would be harder to pass off as the real stuff. "Gosh," she said. "I don't have any straws or little umbrellas." She plopped a piece of lemon into both glasses. Then she aggressively folded two paper napkins and put them, along with the glasses, on a serving tray. "Here. Tell them I'd send some hors d'oeuvres, but I'm all out."

I carried the tray in like a dolt and immediately noticed that something had changed. The lighting for one. It was definitely dimmer, or maybe that was the tunnel vision I was experiencing. I had broken a spell as I entered the family room. Their conversation had taken a detour from athletics—or imagined athletics—to something that I was not welcome to hear. I set the tray down, feeling heavily conspicuous, like I had just carried a pastry tray into Kelly's body-sculpting class. There's a special injustice in doing what you're told to do and then being resented for doing it. No one said a word, and I knew I was expected to turn around and walk back out. Leaving the room, I for some reason had this crazy hope that someone would ask where I was going. Neither one of them did.

Set adrift, I went back to my room for lack of a better place to go. My friend was here at my new house for the first time and he was visiting someone else. Marco had never been to Frank's because I had always come to him. I knew better than to put up with this kind of rejection, but once you accept a role, how do you give it back?

I should have stopped helping Marco last year after he and I got caught cheating in earth science. It wasn't really cheating, or so I had rationalized, if you look at it like I was the smart one tutoring the slow one. Mr. Klingborn knew better. Marco and I would sometimes go into the classroom after eating lunch—that is, Marco at his table and me with Peter, Gretchen, and Anthony at another. I did have some limits—if he was going to copy my homework, he had to do it himself, and he was not getting it in front of a bunch of people. Anyway, like a couple of dopes, we went to the earth science classroom, where Marco copied my homework questions from the end of the chapter. He couldn't do this alone because he needed to comment on my handwriting ("You write like a girl.") and complain that he couldn't make out this word or that word. So he was stealing with my permission, when who should walk into his own classroom but Mr. Klingborn. I couldn't even lie when he asked if Marco was copying.

"Well, I guess I'll have to give both you boys a zero," he said casually, like my whole life wasn't jammed in the toilet by that remark. Then he looked at me with sort of a wry smile and said, "Tristan, you really need to think better of yourself."

Marco said to him, "He was helping me with it." Later when I wanted to talk about it—babble in fear is more like it—Marco laughed.

"Relax," he said. "He doesn't care. He's not going to do anything."

I was so deep into this memory that I'd forgotten there was still dinner to go. Mom and Frank had doctored a few cans of vegetable soup to make it look less like it was from cans, and there was a small dish of whole-cranberry sauce, which had probably been sitting there since the Pilgrims overlooked it that first Thanksgiving. There was also a makeshift bowl of salad with a glaring variety of vegetables in it, along with some kind of whole-grain crackers that could have been corrugated cardboard.

But Marco and Kelly might as well have been alone at dinner. Kelly had this way of making you realize you were not supposed to be talking by not looking at you and then responding with a totally different topic.

After dinner I suffered through Saturday night TV, knowing that Marco and Kelly both wanted me gone. I didn't know what else to do with myself.

It was stupid, I know, but I was brooding over Kelly not volunteering to take me for a walk again. While I didn't want her to take me for a walk, even more I didn't want her *not* to take me for a walk because of Marco. She had promised to make me thin, and hadn't she said she always kept a promise?

Finally, Mom mercifully put an end to the evening.

"Well, Marco, I think it's time for you to head home."

"I don't have to be home yet," he said.

"Until you get your night license, you can't drive past nine without a parent."

"Oh, my parents don't care if I drive past nine."

"I do," Mom said.

"I have my parents' permission," he said, sounding meek for him.

"Doesn't matter. It would be irresponsible of me to let you stay knowing you were breaking the law. I'd be no more likely to let you drink and drive." There was an absoluteness in her voice. But she added, just to make sure, "Come on. Time to go."

Though Marco always had on his slickest manners around my parents, he found it hard to hide his irritation this time. "My parents know I'm a safe driver," he said, but got up anyway. Kelly brushed past us with Marco, and they walked to the back porch together. I went to my room, 8:45 not being too early for a partying fool to go to bed. I figured I wasn't going to be able to sleep—maybe never again—but reading would take up some time so I lay down. At first I slipped into pouting again, but got bored with it and turned to my book, which I got lost in, forgetting the real world.

Then I heard thunderous voices—Frank and Kelly's voices were coming from the kitchen, but in distortion, blaring and scary. I had never heard Frank shout. He was frantic about something.

"This is not about Anne," he said, referring to

my mother. "This is about you, and your doing something illegal and dangerous."

Kelly shouted back, "It's not like he was drinking. We just took a ride."

"He wasn't supposed to be driving after nine, and you knew that because Anne said it right in front of you."

"Anne, Anne, Anne. Is Anne my mother?"

"That's not the point. The point is he isn't allowed to drive at night. *She* didn't say anything about you. *I'm* the one saying you are not allowed to drive with him at night. Me, your father."

"It was half an hour. And all we did was drive around. You don't trust me, that's your problem. You're still mad because I said you gained weight."

"It was defiance. Plain and simple. You knew he was supposed to go right home and put that car away. You just had to show us who was boss."

She mimicked him: "'Put that car away. You just had to show us who was boss.' Good-bye, Dad. Take me to the train station right now."

Frank lowered his voice slightly. "Tomorrow morning, bright and early. You're not taking a train in the middle of the night."

"Then I'll walk."

Mom stuck her head into my room. She was wearing a faded long nightshirt that a man would wear to bed. Her hair was reminiscent of a Halloween witch.

"So how do they compare to me and your father?" she whispered.

"In decibels? I'd say pretty equal. Frank's scary when he's mad."

"She's scary when she's not."

"So she took off with Marco?"

"Yep. Saw him to the door, then saw him through the door, then into his passenger door." She paused. "I think Marco might be persona non grata around here for a while. Maybe forever, or until Kelly's gone. Whichever comes first."

"Great. I have one friend and she gets him evicted."

"You have more than one friend. Besides, Frank won't mind Marco when Kelly's gone."

"But will Marco mind me when Kelly's gone?"

"What?"

"Nothing."

"I don't like that, whatever it means, Tri."

I shrugged.

"It sounds like the worst is over," she said. "Although I did hear him call her 'young lady.' That's always bad news."

"Good night, Mom."

She gave me a rare bashful smile. I wondered if she was embarrassed at what she had gotten us into. "Night."

I didn't bother to stay up for any more fun, figuring that it was really none of my business whether Kelly stayed or not. The problem would be Marco next Monday. I knew that the temperature had been altered and global changes were ahead. The wind that had kept us sailing smoothly probably couldn't be trusted any longer.

Chapter 7

I was expecting big fallout from Marco about the driving-after-nine fiasco, some attitude anyway, or a few token slaps upside the head. Instead of abusing me, however, Marco pretended like nothing had happened. He continued to talk about how hot Kelly was, and to tell other guys about "this girl I'm seeing from Buffalo" who was a junior and, somehow, a model. He didn't even exclude me from the story, trying to raise my stock price by making sure people knew she was my stepsister. I didn't correct him, because the facts never got in Marco's way.

For the most part, my life appeared to be back the way it was before Kelly had touched shore.

I went back and forth between Dad's and Mom's. As for Frank, I sensed, but wasn't sure, that he was not as nice to me afterward. He didn't react as often to my plays on words or other amusing things I prided myself on. Maybe he was just getting used to me being around and didn't feel the need to be as polite anymore. Either way, his not responding made me more cautious when I spoke to him.

This somberness lifted after a few weeks. While things were definitely more like they had been, they were not exactly the same. Maybe it was because we had all experienced The Kelly together and separately, and afterward it was like we were trying to make sense of something that couldn't really be understood.

As it turned out, things went crazy again. I don't know exactly what happened, but one night about eleven Frank got a call. I was kind of alarmed because he sounded so upset I was afraid someone had died. After a minute or so, I started to feel like a jerk for being so nosy and stopped listening in.

Unfortunately, the next day Mom made the special effort of driving me to school instead of to the bus stop near Dad's. She had to break some news to me.

"Kelly's moving in for a while," she said.

"What happened?"

"She's Frank's daughter, Tristan," she growled. "I can't say no."

"Mom, easy. I just asked what happened."

"Sorry." She took an irritable breath. "She got in a big fight with her mother. What a surprise. She can't get along with her mother either. That woman must be a saint."

"That woman must be a pharmacist. What were they fighting about?"

"What does Kelly fight about?" Mom snapped again. "The wind, the trees, a paper cut she got when she was five. I don't know. Maybe her mother ordered a pizza with bacon."

"Well, don't take it out on me."

"I'm not . . ." Then she stopped, looked over at me. "I *am* taking it out on you. I'm sorry. It's just that this really changes everything. Frank and I weren't in any big rush about anything, and all of a sudden I'm the wicked stepmother."

"Well, you were always wicked," I said. "This is just a new opportunity."

"Thanks, son."

"Maybe it won't be so bad. Kelly's got an aerobics class every day of the week, so she'll be home about an hour a day. As long as you clean up after her and don't get in her way, everything will be fine."

"Funny. She is insufferable, no doubt about it. She can put that on her résumé."

"Marco can, too. He's good at facts, if you don't mind fiction."

She pulled up in front of the school.

"Does he still call it 'friction'?" she asked.

"Friction and nonfriction. I don't bother to correct him anymore."

"Give me a kiss, hon," she said. She grabbed me and planted a smacker on my forehead.

"Not in front of the cool people, Mom. They'll think we're functional or something."

"I love you."

"Love you. Go away." She took off and I went in.

Marco was waiting for me after homeroom.

"Kelly's moving here," he said. "Dude, this is incredible."

"How do you know?"

He punched my arm. "How do you think?"

How do you think? could be a literal question coming from Marco, but I gave him the benefit of the doubt. "Have you been talking to her all this time?" I asked.

"No," he answered sarcastically.

So that was that. My arm was throbbing and the conversation was depressing me. "Did you do any studying for the test in English?" I asked.

"No," he answered with the same sarcasm.

"How are you gonna pass?"

"I need special services," he said.

"What kind?"

"A reader. My parents think I need a reader and a note taker."

"But that'll leave me without a job."

"I'm just gonna tell Mr. Rylant that I can't understand any of it. They're not supposed to do that book in tenth grade anyway."

"What learning disorder are you trying out today?"

"I think I have dyslexia nervosa."

"Sounds serious," I said. "Can't eat and can't read?"

"When you have dyslexia, you see everything backward," Marco said.

"Then how come you don't drive on the wrong side of the road and backward?"

"I do. When I have a hot babe in the car with me."

Sometimes Marco was quicker than I gave him credit for being.

Frank picked up Kelly in Buffalo and I helped him haul in her luggage and boxes. She was more radiant than ever, and she was not the least bit embarrassed about her reason for being back.

73

The first thing she said when she saw me was, "Tristan, you look like you've lost some weight! You look great!"

This kind of compliment hinges on the idea that you need to lose weight in the first place and that you should lose more. But because she was so gorgeous and fragrant and commanding, I'm afraid I beamed a little. Once again I had the impulse to do anything for her if she asked me.

Neither Mom nor Frank was as cheery as Kelly. Frank looked like he was constipated with his grim, pained line of a mouth. Mom was friendly in a careful way. If she noticed anything, Kelly didn't say so.

"It's so good to be home again," she said. "Dad, I can hardly wait to get to school. And now I can visit all my old friends from Putnam because they'll be nearby." Putnam was the school district that Frank's house was in, and the one I had been spared transferring to because of Dad's moving into our old house.

"But won't you be going to Putnam?" Mom asked. She looked apprehensive.

"Oh no. That's my agreement with Dad. I told him if I was going to come back here, I had to go to Green Hills, because going back to Putnam would bring back too many memories. It would be like starting all over again there, and I don't want to."

"So . . ."

"So, he has to pay some tuition, but it's not a big deal. Green Hills is better anyway. Academically. Everyone says so. And there's a better phys ed program all around."

Kelly would be at my school. Marco was at my school.

"Marco's gonna be glad to see you," I said. I didn't mean for it to be instigating, just something that would make her feel good. But the room froze like an ice age had ambushed it.

"We've had a talk about this Marco," Frank said in that deep, menacing voice, which at the same time sounded a little pleading. "I think he's too freewheeling for his age. Kelly knows my feelings about him and knows to keep her distance. He won't be visiting us until he can prove he's matured."

"Oh," I said, wondering where Marco would buy this proof.

"I know what I'm doing," Kelly said, ending the subject. "Dad and I are going in early so I can register. Also, we're getting him a gym membership. That's part of our deal, too."

Kelly's first order of business that night was to give me a nutrition lecture. She sat on my bed. "Let's talk carbohydrates," she said. "Carbs can be good and bad. Carbs provide us with energy, but Americans don't need that much energy! For instance, rice is a carb, brown rice and long grain rice are carbs, but so is a slice of pizza. So is a piece of chocolate cake with frosting. You could run fifty miles on that kind of energy, but most people don't run fifty miles after a piece of cake, do they?" She looked at me with her gigantic, beautiful eyes, and for a second I thought I might kiss her, just to try it, although I would have to set myself on fire afterward. "Do you know, Tristan, people think they can eat sugar-free products to lose weight? Look in the grocery store. Big, luscious chocolate cakes, all sugar free. And guess what's wrong with them?"

"They give you diarrhea?"

She winced. "They're full of carbs! Simple carbs! If there's flour in that cake there are carbs in that cake, so who are they kidding?"

"I don't know."

"Neither do I. So, back to the good carbs." She went on to explain to me the glories of whole wheat, unprocessed breads, and certain vegetables

76

that were carbohydrates. Then she lashed into white bread, junk food, nachos. By the time she was finished, she had paraded before my imagination every wonderful food that had ever existed, and I was ready to eat.

At the end of the lecture, she yawned, told me she had to go make a call, and left. There would be no walking tonight. Probably she was going to call the freewheeling Marco.

I had to ride in the next morning with Kelly and Frank. Although I was excited about being seen with her, I was afraid of what being seen with me was going to do to her. I could have been wrong, but I thought I saw Marco's Accord parked correctly in the student lot as we went in. On any other occasion this would have been a mirage because Marco not only never came to school early, he was still home designing his hair well into first period. But as I was to learn, there were lots of things that Marco didn't tell me anymore.

Chapter 8

Fairness comes in small lumps. Unfairness comes in barrels. It only took Kelly one week at my school to become the center of attention. She and Marco were like royalty. I'd been at Green Hills since forever and hardly anyone knew my name. But all she had to do was show up and people were all over her. And Marco was her king-consort. Being her boyfriend gave him that final ascent to the top of the class—not academically, of course, because nothing had that much power. Although I lived with Kelly every other week, my net gain on the social scale was zero.

One day while I was walking down the hall toward bio, a school photographer was snapping a picture of Kelly and Marco for the yearbook. In the picture you can see me in the background, trying to hold my books and push hair out of my eyes at the same time, one of those stupid "What's going on?" looks on my face. You would not think this klutz in the shadows had anything in common with them, but rather that he had walked into the picture from another life.

Kelly would speak to me at school, and that was something. Every day when she saw me in the hall the first time, she would say, "Hey." Of course that was that for the day. If I passed her a thousand more times, I was as unnoticeable as a row of lockers.

Things with Marco and me had finally made it all the way around that corner we'd been turning. There had been some clues. Now when he called Frank's, he was only looking for Kelly. He had to be sneaky, asking for me if Mom or Frank answered. I called him a couple of times to try to get myself invited over, but he'd barely pay attention to me when he found out Kelly wasn't around. Yet for some reason, I still held on to a rickety hope that he would come around. I thought maybe he would crumble during bio lab when he realized he would have to break in another servant. But when Mr. Finn had us test the sugar in our urine, Marco worked with Tara Montoya. She was really beautiful, sweet, and nice, and I had a life-long crush on her, which I showed by turning completely red whenever she walked by. But she wasn't a serf. She might do the bulk of the work for him this time, but probably not again. Maybe he would come back begging when he understood how inconvenient it was to get good help.

With Kelly around all the time, Frank was tense and tight-lipped. Once he even yelled at me for leaving the door open when it was cold. "Close the door," he said, and his voice had an angry intensity. He growled in a lower tone, "We're not heating the outdoors, you know."

But that night he made a special effort to apologize. "So, I'm sorry," he said, his big hand on my shoulder. For just a second I had the impulse to hug him but decided against it.

Yet things didn't go back the way they had been with him after our tender moment. He stayed removed and sad. Every once in a while he and Kelly would flare up, and there would be a fight behind closed doors.

Kelly was also making our principal's life a little harder. When she drove Frank's car to school, she parked nearly sideways, prompting more lectures during the announcements.

"If you can't park a car between two lines, you shouldn't be driving at all. I don't care how expensive your car is, that does not give you permission to take up more than one space.

Parking privileges will be suspended for all students if all students do not cooperate. Cooperate!"

I went to my classes and came home. I had my band friends, but they weren't very interesting to me lately. Then something happened with them that I didn't see coming. While I was distracted by Marco slipping away and his and Kelly's rise to the stratosphere, my band friends were living their lives in forward. I went on eating with Peter and Anthony and Gretchen, though I often stole uneasy glances over at the table where Marco and my beautiful sort of sister sat with the cool and the powerful. Clearly, I wasn't paying enough attention to where I was actually sitting, because one day I noticed Anthony and Gretchen holding hands, like it was nothing new. I pretended not to be surprised, didn't ask any questions. But the rest of the afternoon I was obsessed with it. When had this happened? Why hadn't I noticed before? And, most annoyingly, why was I jealous? I'd never even thought of Gretchen that way, as someone I would want to go out with even if she wanted to go out with me. It had never occurred to me that she was anything other than one of the guys. And Anthony wasn't the kind of person I expected to have a girlfriend. Yet they sat there in full view of the world, showing off their love. Fortunately they didn't make out or anything, but they looked completely relaxed with each other.

Later when I saw Peter alone I asked him about it.

"So, when did Anthony and Gretch start going out?"

He shrugged, no big deal to him. "A few weeks, maybe."

"I didn't even know he liked her. Or she liked him."

"I guess they like each other."

"So, did he ask her out or something?"

Peter sounded annoyed by this inquisition. "I don't know. I didn't ask."

"Well, why not? How did it happen?"

He looked at me. "Didn't your parents ever have that talk with you? What do you mean how did it happen?"

"I mean," I said, starting to feel more and more foolish but no less obsessed, "like, they were just friends and now they're going out."

"It happens, you know," he said. He changed the subject. "My mom's boyfriend is getting wireless. We can get on-line anywhere in the house."

"Cool," I said, but I couldn't shake myself to a new topic. "Are they . . . do they talk about what's going on?"

"Who? What are you talking about?"

"Anthony and Gretchen. Are they serious or just dating or stuff like that?"

"They're not getting married," he said. "Why do you care? Did you want to go out with her?"

"No," I said so hard that you might think I meant yes, which I didn't.

"So?"

"So? So I'm surprised, that's all. No one said anything. They never talked about it."

"You don't really pay attention," he said, then clobbered me good with, "You're always chasing Marco Cavi around. Hey, your stepsister is really cute, by the way. I wish a girl like that would go out with me. She's gorgeous."

"Thanks," I said, like it had anything to do with me.

Chapter 9

There was more yogurt in our Thanksgiving dinner than in the mountains of Russia where people live hundreds of years eating it. There was more yogurt than in southern California where people bathe in it. Kelly wasn't much for domestic things, but the idea of Thanksgiving dinner had suddenly brought her to life the way washing dishes didn't.

"This is going to be the healthiest Thanksgiving ever," she stated, with authentic enthusiasm. She didn't use the word *best* because I think in some deep recess of her mind, she knew that *healthiest* and *best* were contradictory when applied to a Thanksgiving dinner. "Dad and I will go shopping. I'm going to make a new man of him."

Frank came back from the store looking like he needed a cigarette. I helped him and Kelly carry in endless plastic bags of groceries, and Frank vanished. Figuring my part was done, too, I headed back to my homework, but Kelly stopped me.

"Tristan, wait. There are a bunch of things I want to show you here." She pulled out a bag of what looked like sugar, but the bag was too small and had yellowed, low-budget printing on it. "Fructose," she announced. "This is what's in fruit." I must have looked confused because she added, "The sugar in fruit? So it doesn't get in your bloodstream so fast, like refined sugar, which shocks the system immediately."

"Are you sure you're not diabetic?" I asked, joking.

"No," she flared, "I'm not. Just because I take care of myself doesn't mean I've got a disease. Just think of all the people in this world who would not have health problems if they paid attention to some simple facts."

Then, wishing I had a mute button for my mouth, I said, "You're in really, really great . . . you know . . . shape, and all."

My face must have been blushing till it throbbed, because Kelly softened right away. "You're so sensitive," she said. "I'm just explaining things to you. Okay, so, the dessert this Thanksgiving? I'm making it with fructose. Your body will thank you. You won't be able to tell the difference. I swear."

She took out a few more bags of fructose and handed them to me. "Help me put these away." She smiled, and I knew that shouldn't be reward enough even though it was. "Next, we have yogurt. Plain yogurt." She took out of the bag a plastic tub that looked like it should have ricotta cheese in it. "Instead of clogging up your arteries with dairy, we're going to use yogurt."

I wanted to ask her what she thought of Marco's refrigerator, full to the brim with homemade lasagne, Italian pastries, fancy cheeses, and cake. Instead, fine memories of those better days with Marco doused me with sadness. No matter how beautiful Kelly was, and no matter how I needed her approval despite all the reasons not to, I couldn't help but feel she had stolen my friend away from me. It was stupid and illogical and melodramatic. It was true.

"Yogurt instead of butter," she continued. "I know how to substitute yogurt for butter in recipes, and I know how to make a spread with yogurt for rolls."

"Isn't yogurt dairy?" I asked.

"It won't kill you," she snarled again. "If you buy the right kind, yogurt has no fat whatsoever." Then, possibly because she realized she had yelled at me twice in two minutes, she said, "Tristan, can I confide in you?"

"Yeah, I guess so."

"I'm so worried about my father. What would you do if your father just dropped dead?"

I had no response, but that was her point.

"Stick with me, kid," she said. "We'll have those extra pounds off you in no time."

"Oh," I said.

"And it's not just what's on the outside that's important," she said. "It's what's inside that counts most. For you, it's the perfect time. If things don't get out of control for you now, you'll never wind up like Dad." I pictured Frank—tall, handsome, successful.

Luckily, I had an escape hatch for Thanksgiving. I was going to spend Thanksgiving day with Mom, and late afternoon and evening with my dad and Cyndi and some friends of theirs. When they were together, my parents had always fought about when to eat dinner on holidays. My mother insisted on two o'clock. My father wanted a nighttime, candlelit thing, the culmination of the day. We usually had visitors, too, like Mom's sister, my aunt Linda, and her husband, Den, and sometimes Den's son. Often there was a friend of my parents from the university, usually a person from their department who was new in town and needed a family for the day.

Now Mom didn't dare invite anyone over because Kelly had co-opted Thanksgiving. So I was looking forward to a traditional meal at Dad's and thinking of how hard it was going to be to smile through Kelly's rendition without gagging.

I had happy olfactory memories of waking up on Thanksgiving morning with the smell of roasting turkey filling the house. But on this Thanksgiving I woke up to no such homeyness. I heard noises in the kitchen and decided to check out what it could be. It was just Mom and Frank eating breakfast.

"What time are we eating?" I asked, trying not to sound as anxious as the question made me.

"I told Kelly we had to eat by two since you're leaving at five for your father's."

"Oh, okay." I already knew this, but I was surprised that at 9:30 in the morning, the cook would not have begun at least some preliminaries for a dinner at two. I considered asking if the turkey was in the oven, but since I had not seen one brought in after the shopping the other night, and since Kelly hated animal fats, I didn't want my worst fears confirmed.

The day trickled by, and still I smelled nothing from the kitchen. I passed through a couple times to steal a granola bar or an apple, and there was no sign of pots or pans being moved around for the greater good. Finally I heard Frank knock on Kelly's door and tell her gently that she had to get up. This was noon. A half hour later I heard him knock again, and by about one Kelly made her way out of the shower.

"We're hungry, girl," her father said with as fake a good cheer as I'd ever heard. "Where's our Thanksgiving dinner?"

"Perfection can't be rushed," she said with her pitiless smile, and walked back to her room, not rushing. She must have made the journey from her bedroom to the kitchen at some point, because there were noises, and there were scents of things baking, though no roasting turkey in the mix. Valuing my life as I did, I didn't ask her when dinner might be done, and there was no sneaking into the kitchen because she was reigning supreme there. I later found out that she had wanted me to help, but since both Mom and Frank had been scolded for their incompetence while trying to cook with her, I hadn't been drafted. Instead, we waited, entertaining ourselves in ways that weren't very entertaining.

Finally, at 4:30, Kelly beckoned Mom to get the table set.

"Things are almost ready," she said. "I just need to carve the tofu."

That sounded ominous.

"I've got to take Tristan to his father's in fifteen minutes, hon," Mom said, obviously trying to hide her irritation.

"Oh, come on," Kelly said playfully. "Just have a little, Tristan. It's the best meal you're ever going to have. Your father won't mind. And it's for a good cause. You!"

"No," Mom answered. "We have an agreement and I have to stick to it, especially on holidays."

Kelly turned, disregarding her. Then she called to me, "At least help me with the turkey, Tristan. You can have a piece before you go."

Mom and I looked at each other. Turkey? Had one been air-dropped by a Red Cross plane? Was Kelly a magician? I toddled into the kitchen. In a roasting pan lay a brown-gray miniature turkey. It smelled a little like corn dogs.

"This," she said proudly, "is the, quote, turkey."

"Wow," I said, really meaning it, too, because this was the first clay turkey I'd even seen.

"It's soy," she said. "This is the great thing about healthy food. You get to be a sculptor, too!" Then, as

I watched without helping at all, Kelly very deftly placed little white paper frills on the ends of the makeshift legs, which was a nice touch because they disguised the fact that the legs came to sharp points.

"I'd carve out a hole for the stuffing," she said, "but I'm afraid it will collapse." I laughed hard for her, an effort she ignored. "Well, this is what you're missing. Not one ounce of artery-clogging animal fat and no preservatives or hormones."

"Sounds good," I said, then waited for my mother to insist it was time to go.

"Here," she said, grabbing a knife. "Just have a piece before you go."

"Oh, that's okay. I'm going to my father's," I said, but Kelly already had a piece of brown stuff up to my mouth. I ate it out of her hand.

"Mmm, good," I said in that false tone I had become accustomed to using with her. But it was good, really good, unexpectedly good. It was more of a bread than a meat, which made sense since it wasn't meat. It was rich and had kind of a nutty, dark flavor.

"See, Tristan?" Kelly said. "I'm not all bad, am I?"

"No. I mean, uh, you're not bad all the time. I mean, at all. You know . . ."

She laughed. "Foods that are good for you can be good food," she said, and smiled in a friendly way. I looked into her brilliant eyes and smiled back. For the first time we had an unguarded moment.

"Tristan, let's go," Mom said, breaking the unguarded moment in half as she blitzed through the kitchen, putting on her coat. "It's starting to snow. Wear a hat. Go ahead and serve, Kelly," she said. My mother always tried to be even around Kelly, but she couldn't help giving commands.

The snowflakes were falling thick and fast, and Mom said in the car, "Well, it looks like a blizzard. I guess I'll have to stay at your father's tonight."

"Not to mention we're having a real roast turkey," I said.

"You can just throw me table scraps."

"Oh, come on, Mom. You know they'll let you sit at the kiddie table."

By the time we got to Dad's, the world was shrouded in winter.

"Mom, it's snowing hard. Maybe you really should stay here."

"I'll be okay. I'll drive slowly. Maybe I'll stop at the diner on the way home, then tell Frank and Kelly I got stuck in a ditch."

"How will you explain being full?"

"I'll tell her soy turkey is one of my binge foods and will trigger my eating disorder," she said. "That ought to get me out of it."

After she dropped me off, I stood outside. I couldn't go in right away because I couldn't swallow the lump in my throat. You're too old to cry like a baby, I said to myself. I was here for a good time with Dad and Cyndi, but I had to send my mother away in the dark in a snowstorm to a strange meal with someone she didn't like very much. When Mom and Dad first got divorced, I used to get annoyed at hearing about kids who never gave up the fantasy that their parents would get back together. But now I was standing in the dark and the snow trying to figure some way that Mom could join us in our old house where a real turkey was roasting and people were having fun. Finally I gave up, swallowed as many times as I could, and wiped my eyes. It was Dad's first candlelit Thanksgiving dinner. I wouldn't ruin it.

Chapter 10

Kelly had decided not to spend any part of the holidays in Buffalo, not even Christmas Day. Frank told me this news like he was holding a post-assassination press conference. Then he added, "Merry Christmas."

This situation may have resulted from Kelly's typical phone conversations with her mother. Her tone would begin reasonably, then mutate into a tirade. Tirades are, by definition, very loud. The pre-Christmas fight must have lasted three hours.

"Why would you say that?" she'd bellowed into the receiver. "Why would you say that to me? I would never talk to a person again who said that to me. Do you think just because you're my mother you can say anything?"

There was silence on our end for a few seconds while her mother presumably defended herself. Then Kelly, having waited too long as it was, exploded again.

If I hadn't heard the word *mother*, I would have sworn it was Frank on the other end. Kelly might as well have taped her lectures and saved herself the trouble of giving them over and over.

A tiny bud of pity for her built in my mind, which countered the fearful respect I usually held.

Feeling a little sorry for Kelly didn't mean being safe around her. I could barely eat anything when she was around without feeling her eyes weighing on me. One night after a typical dessertless dinner, I decided to have a couple of oatmeal cookies and a glass of milk before taking on my math homework. I dimmed the kitchen lights and quietly put my milk on the table, keeping an ear open for predators. Then, silent as a panther, I reached in the bread drawer where the cookies were and felt for two. Kelly was quieter, because I turned around and there she was, a knowing look on her face. She turned the lights up. We locked eyes for a second, and I put the cookies back and shut the drawer, my hands shaking. Kelly got a yogurt out of the refrigerator, then left, and I sat at the kitchen table drinking milk until I couldn't stand it, as if that had been my intention all along. Neither of us had said a word.

The day school let out for Christmas vacation I came home with frosted, scented candles with various

Christmas scenes on them, which we'd been selling in band for a month. I had three left and felt that it was wrong to turn them back in, knowing I could pawn them off on Mom or Dad, maybe some of the neighbors. I thought they were kind of attractive, fat and tall, lots of wax for a buck. I had a small variety, one with Santa, one with three solemn candles burning, and one with a skating scene.

Gretchen had given Peter and me a hug and kiss on the cheek before we left for the day, and for some reason I couldn't get it out of my head. She was still going out with Anthony and I only liked her as a friend, but it still got me confused. She was kind of goofy looking with her big white-braces smile and her thousand freckles. Probably she was just being a good friend, better than I deserved. If by some chance she wanted to be more than a friend, I guess she would have to fight off Tara Montoya and all the other girls for me.

And why wouldn't girls fight over me with the picture I made coming through the kitchen door in my usual clumsy manner, weighed down by my box of candles, my French horn, my books? Dad had dropped me off at the beginning of Frank's drive-way, which was at least an eighth of a mile downhill from the house. By the time I was in the door my cheeks must have been red as roses. As I passed the family room, there was a Christmas surprise that I could have lived without: Marco and Kelly were sitting there, as close as three dimensions would allow. Kelly was giggling.

"Seen your eat-a," Marco said, tickling her. Kelly giggled again, then noticed me.

"Dude," Marco offered.

"We're studying Spanish," said Kelly, who was taking French. And so—to the extent that he took any subject—was Marco.

"Oh, okay."

"What are you staring at?" she asked, almost good-natured.

"Nothing."

"Take a picture, it'll last longer," she said.

"Dude, what's in the box?" Marco asked with a smirk.

"Um, dude, candles."

"Let's see them."

I left my other stuff on the floor to obey the command. I brought the box in. Marco took the candles, one by one, and laughed.

"Ugly," he said, rotating the candle scene for

the full panoramic effect. "What are you selling these for?"

A few lies skittered through my head—the homeless, abused children, the rain forest—but all I could scrape together was, "Band."

"You should tell the director you refuse to sell this crap," he said, spitting the condescension out like it was bitter. "Look at these." He handed the Santa to Kelly.

"It's kind of cute," she said.

"Piece of garbage," he said.

"It's a candle, Marco," she said.

"Band is so lame." Marco had played the cornet for exactly one week in seventh grade until he realized taking band meant learning to read music and losing a study hall.

Kelly asked, "How many did you sell?"

"Just a few." I had sold twenty-seven.

"Oh, well, for a good cause," she said, putting them back in the box.

"What's the good cause?" Marco asked.

"Uh, uniforms, I think," I said.

Kelly smiled. "Well let's hope there's something with a cape." Marco shrieked laughter.

That was as good a cue as any to get lost. I took the box and gathered my other stuff. I went into my room. I spent way too much time there when I was at Frank's. A sacrilegious thought crossed my mind about living with Dad full-time. It would hurt Mom, but it might come down to that. Even if Cyndi had a baby, I would be thirty by the time it called me "dude." By then I would probably have my own place, and I wouldn't be selling candles for band uniforms anymore.

I hid the candles as far back in my closet as they would go and camouflaged them with some sweaters. Until I thought of a way to smuggle them back out of the house, they were staying hidden, my ugly little secret.

Dad had wanted an old photo album for Cyndi, so he could show her what he used to look like when he was her age. The best place to look was the attic, where I could occupy myself until Kelly and Marco were done lamenting the decline of good taste, and in Spanish no less. Frank's house was fairly new, so the attic wasn't spooky or old, and it was accessible from the closet in the upstairs hallway. There was a partially finished floor, and a six-foot-wide walk space of wooden planks down the center of the attic. On either side were wooden frame joists about a foot or so apart, the spaces between them filled with fiberglass insulation.

I looked around for a box where the album might be packed away.

At first glance, there didn't appear to be one obvious starting place to look. There was junk from two families, piled high and haphazard.

Frank had some old wooden crates to store stuff. I opened one and was immediately disappointed—just a bunch of old clothes. I pulled out an old white sweater with ugly red embroidery. Then, feeling bad—it wasn't mine to look at—I tried to fold it neatly to put it back. Underneath it, however, was something unusual, an old, drab, brown cloak that could have been worn by Hagrid from *Harry Potter*. For some reason, it was one of those things that said, "Play with me," at least to a history-mad, candle-hoarding, French horn player.

The cloak had that forlorn attic smell. I slipped it on and was bathed in scratchy material and dust. Maybe I looked like the Grim Reaper. Then I remembered Mrs. Junker's description of Mary,

Queen of Scots's execution, when her wig came off as the executioner was trying to hold up her severed head. "Mary knew how to embarrass her enemies," Mrs. Junker had said. The rest of the class had been grossed out, but I was mesmerized. Embarrassing your enemies—that was a skill I could stand to learn while I still had my head.

So, wearing the cloak, I pretended I was the executioner.

"Madam," I said in a grave tone. "It is time." I felt sorry for her, considering what she was about to lose. Still I admired the survivors, too, people like Henry VIII's daughter Elizabeth I, who had, not incidentally, signed the warrant for this beheading. She knew something about survival, which was definitely better than a heroic death.

"So endeth the troubles of Mary Stuart." I balanced myself on the wooden joists, feeling silly and completely childlike, free of any worry. Standing on two parallel joists toward the imaginary victim, I held the ax over my head for the chop.

Then I was stuck numb in that position—this silly, childlike freedom now a frozen mass of shame. What an idiot I was. When we were little, Marco and I explored his attic like it was a huge treasure chest. Now, in tenth grade, I was still playing in the attic. Why was I so weird?

Nothing could make me feel more like a loser, that is, until my left foot slipped off the joist onto the insulation. In a panic I tried to correct myself, but my right foot slipped off the other side of the beam. There was one second of stillness, before the ceiling beneath me gave way.

Things had broken beneath me before: a porch step; a lawn chair; and once sitting alone on one side of a picnic table, I stood up and my side shot into the air while the people on the other side fell to the ground.

But how do I describe the sensation of falling through a floor? There's a suspension of time when something collapses beneath you, a second or two where you don't know what's happening and you can't speak. All I know is that when I did come to, my legs, up to the gonads, had been flushed into the room below. I had fallen through the house.

Insulation fibers and dust were making me choke. My butt had landed solid on the joist, so I knew I wouldn't fall anymore. It wasn't just my butt that had made contact, but my whole bike-seat area. *Ouch* doesn't quite define it.

There might have been some dignity in falling all the way through and winding up in a wheelchair, but at this point dignity was not within reach. With the first shock passed, I wondered which room my legs and feet were dangling into. If it was a bedroom, I would be discovered eventually, and the circle of humiliation would be complete. But luck might be on my side and the joist itself would give way so the jagged edges of Sheetrock could rip my head off. That would be poetic justice for Miss Stuart.

Then I heard noise below me. The door to the attic opened and Marco and Kelly pounded up the stairs. I tried curling my legs up toward me in desperate attempts at freeing myself, but they hung like meat in a butcher's window. I had to get the damn cloak off—I could *not* be found wearing that. It would be better to be found naked than to be found playing dress up. But the skirt of the cloak had gotten wedged into the building materials.

Marco was first to reach the edge of the safe plank floor. "What the hell? Dude! Oh, my God, he committed sewer-side! Dude, it was just a candle!"

Kelly looked down at the half of me. "Tristan, what happened? Are you okay?"

I gave her a weak smile.

Kelly spoke again. "Did you hear me? Are you okay? What are you wearing?"

"Hey," I said, and blew a little insulation out of my mouth.

This scene could have played itself out in different ways. For example, Marco and Kelly could have been on Kelly's bed and I could have fallen on top of them, which could have put all three of us on the front page of the local paper. Or I could have shouted for help and then later claimed that I had been ignored, and pressed charges against Kelly and Marco. Or, since people were more likely to come to your aid if there was a blaze than if they heard a generic cry for help, I could have yelled "Fire!" and maybe one of Frank's neighbors from three acres away would hear me, get me loose, and be bribed not to mention the incident to the *Enquirer.*

Instead, I was rescued immediately and unharmed. Too bad.

Marco braced himself on the two joists from

which I had recently tried to perform my execution-ary duties. He crouched and grabbed me.

"Are there nails?" he demanded, urgent but steady.

"I don't think so." I could feel pricks and points all over my thighs, but they were probably edges of the Sheetrock.

"Be careful, Marco," Kelly said.

"Okay, slow then," he said. He jimmied me by the armpits enough so I could grab onto his shoulders with my hands. I could smell Kelly's perfume through the dust clogging my nose.

"I'm gonna pull. You tell me if you get caught on anything."

"Okay."

"Hold on to the stud in case any more of the ceiling gives way."

"Let me help," Kelly said.

"Grab an arm," he said.

She reached under the cloak for an arm. They were both very strong. The two of them worked hard on me while I acted like I was doing something. But I was an enormous lump, unable to twist or wriggle or squirm. I used to think that I knew what embarrassment was.

At first nothing happened. Then my right leg came free and after that it was as if they were yanking out an easy tooth. Somehow they were able to balance themselves and hold me at the same time. As I recovered enough altitude to lift myself on the joists, Marco held me steady and guided me to my feet. He held on to me as we tightroped along the joists and back to the planked walkway. The cloak was tangled around me.

"What do you have on? What is that thing?" Marco asked.

"An old band uniform, I think."

"Dude, it's a dress."

"It's not a dress."

"What are you doing wearing your mother's old pregnancy gown?"

"It's not a dress, Marco," Kelly said. "It's like a monk's costume or something. Tristan, take it off." She helped me lift it over my head. "Brown's not your color."

I moved for the crate where I'd found it to put it away.

"No," she said, grabbing it and tossing it into a corner. She dusted me off with her hands. "Go clean up."

"What were you doing up here?" Marco asked.

Words filled my throat like jagged marbles. I wasn't skillful like they were at smoothing over the truth. I said the first ridiculous thing that came to mind. "I fell."

"You fell doing what?"

The problem with not dying was I would have to come up with some answers. The relief of not being trapped between floors for a lifetime quickly diminished. "I was looking for something my mom put away up here—"

Kelly shook her head. "Never mind," she said. "Just as long as he's all right." She smiled at me. "You're just like a little brother. I don't suppose you know when your last tetanus shot was."

"No."

"Well, we'd better get you cleaned up and wait for your mother to tell us. Any cuts?"

"I don't think so," I said, thinking maybe my soul had a few rips. I followed as they led the way downstairs. There was so much to be dealt with that I couldn't organize a plan. I hoped there were some serious internal injuries. Nothing to kill me, just enough to take off a lot of heat.

"Marco has to go now," Kelly said. "My father has kind of a problem with him being here. And I don't think your mother would be thrilled either. She gives him a lot of attitude. You'll need to be quiet about it."

I would have sold military secrets for her at that point. "Yes," I said.

"Go in the bathroom, and I'll try to clean up my bedroom. You made a mess. It's a good thing no one was in there when it happened."

I managed to get away from them and into my bathroom. I showered off the dust and insulation first, then drew a warm bath. Kelly had advised me to just use a washcloth and sponge myself because immersing in water would make the scratches sting even more. But I had to soak. All I could see were a few scrapes, no blood. The water seared the broken skin on my hairless legs at first, but eventually soothed me. I washed carefully. I was too blank to know what to expect, and for a few steaming minutes I didn't care.

As I lay back, I could hear the Shop-Vac going in her bedroom. I drained the water and showered off again and dried myself. Kelly had hung my bathrobe on the outside knob of the door. I put it on, then went out in the hall. Kelly's bedroom door was open and I could see that she had already cleaned up the evidence and was sitting calmly in a chair reading *Running Today*.

"I'm sorry," I managed.

"For what?" She smiled, making me wonder if it had all been a TV show. "Nothing happened. That?" she asked, pointing to two ragged holes in the ceiling that gave an interesting perspective on the attic. "I did that. While I was here all alone. I'll take the blame."

My head was too full to completely comprehend, but I knew a deal had been struck.

"But, Tristan," she said. "I hope this encourages you to try to take care of yourself. You know what I mean? *Really* take care of yourself?"

I nodded. I understood. I always understood.

Mom and I put up Frank's artificial Christmas tree that night. I tried to hide my cowboy swagger from her as much as possible, but that region of my body ached like a pain pump had been implanted there.

Mom seemed dispirited about decorating. Kelly and Frank were in the screaming stage of another argument, which I prayed had nothing to do with home improvements. As hard as Mom and I tried, we could not get the lights to work. Finally we gave up.

Mom gave a remote nod. "This is going to be the best Christmas ever. By the way, Tri, why did you want to know about your last tetanus shot?"

"Oh, nothing," I said. Kelly had much to teach me about evasion.

"Tristan, tell me."

"Ma, remember that expression 'Ask me no questions, I'll tell you no lies'?"

"Hmm . . ."

"I'm not very good at quick lying, so ask me no questions anyway."

She grimaced but quit pursuing it.

This was definitely going to be the strangest Christmas I'd ever had. Dad and I would be spending it alone because Cyndi was going to Chicago. At Mom's I would have to do a lot of avoiding of eye contact with Kelly and keep hoping that Frank didn't discover a fat-boy-size hole in her bedroom ceiling. And Kelly might volunteer to make Christmas dinner.

I still had to do more Christmas shopping. What do you give to the people in your life who are not related to you but are forced to live with you anyway?

There was that extra Santa candle.

Chapter 11

This was what it was like to be a little brother, only worse: Kelly and Marco were going cross-country skiing with the new equipment they had gotten for Christmas, and I was tagging along.

The fact that Marco was here at Frank's house in the first place just proved my theory that everything always worked out for him. Frank had not officially forgiven Marco for the driving-after-nine incident, but Kelly used me as a reference when she was arguing for his restoration.

"He's Tristan's friend, for God's sake," she said. "Are you telling Tristan he can't have his friends over to your house? Tell Tristan that." I wanted to stay out of it. Instead, I nodded, backing her up. This was our Montreal.

Frank gave in again: Marco could come over, but it couldn't be a school night and Kelly was not allowed to go to his house at all, since his parents were terrible supervisors.

It hadn't been my idea to go cross-country skiing with them. I had never been cross-country skiing. I used to downhill and had even joined the middle-school ski club, but skiing in high school was about the clothes and being seen, and I felt big and blundering in my clothes. I never went downhill anymore.

Kelly didn't flinch when Mom suggested I go along, though her face froze.

"Well, Anne, it's like this. Marco and I are just friends, and we're just going skiing together. Don't worry about me. I'm a big girl."

"Oh, I'm not worried about you," Mom said with just a little too much fake sincerity. "Marco's Tristan's friend, too, remember? I'm not asking him to chaperone."

"That's good," Kelly said, dropping the forced politeness. "Because I don't need one."

"He's also incidentally my son," Mom said, then tried to smile, giving her the look of someone in intense pain.

Kelly took another position. "This will be such good exercise for him," she said. "I told you I would help you as much as I could, didn't I, Tristan? I'm like your own personal trainer, and free, too."

"Free," I said, shooting Mom a look that should have put out an eye.

When Marco arrived and found out I was making it a threesome, he pretended he didn't hate the idea. So Kelly and Marco took me along, too. They talked to each other in the front seat, occasionally turning and saying something to me, like I was the kid they were baby-sitting and had to keep happy.

When we got to Holt Park, I couldn't get into Frank's skis. Getting into the bindings was more work than should be expected of a beginner. Getting into downhill skis was nothing, but clicking the front of my boots into these bindings required foot-eye coordination I didn't have.

My knobby clothes weren't helping either. Marco and Kelly were in striking dark and bright coordinated, skintight winter outfits and Marco had a backpack as well. I was wearing an old pair of jeans that I hoped would hold out the whole day and a ragwool sweater under my fading brown parka. It may have been a bad omen earlier that morning when the grip on my jeans' zipper broke off. But I had to wear them because my long underwear looked less bulky under those particular jeans. So I got a pair of pliers from Frank's cellar and went to work yanking the zipper. I was sweating by the time I got them zipped, but they were zipped. Fortunately no one was around to see that curious scene, but another Tristan Moment was waiting to happen because after improvising too long with my boots, I had to ask for help. Soon both Marco and Kelly were holding on to one of my feet trying to shove it into the respective binding.

"You've got a death-perception problem," said Marco.

"Depth perception," Kelly corrected, "and no, he doesn't."

Finally there were clicks and Marco patted me. He actually patted me. "There you go, buddy," he said. "It's no big deal. It's just like downhill except you're walking."

As if those words were a starting gun, he and Kelly skied off into the woods. At first I thought I was supposed to keep up with them. I tried taking off in their direction, but found myself stuck in the snow, my legs held in unyielding positions. By the time I managed to get up and get going, I figured that I should get and stay lost. At least I wouldn't have to endure the embarrassment of their waiting for me as I occasionally splattered.

The cross-country skis were much harder to control than downhill skis, and the motion that propelled me seemed silly. When I came to a real hill, I was irritated that I had no control at all, that I couldn't snowplow to stop myself like with mountain skis. After about fifteen minutes, I had the inclination to find my way home, just like the first night Kelly took me for an endurance walk. I had no idea when she and Marco would be ready to leave, or how they would find me when they were, if they even intended to find me at all. Kelly wouldn't dare show up at home without me—Mom would take her head off. But they could be hours and I couldn't stand this another minute.

I could feel tears in my eyes. That would move me ahead socially—Kelly and Marco finding me crying and covered with snow. Of course, that couldn't top finding me in a cassock halfway through the attic floor. I didn't know what to do, so I just moved forward.

The gliding started coming more naturally, and I started to feel a fluid skater's rhythm with each push off. And I also noticed the quiet. It was incredibly still on the trail, a tranquil, soothing stillness, like when I would go into the woods at Frank's house (before hunting season, that is) and just walk until I couldn't see civilization anymore.

Now, because I had stopped focusing on torture, I was feeling alert and alive, as if my racing heart had woken me up to the wonder of my surroundings. I skied on, thinking maybe the day wasn't turning out as hellish as it had promised—there might be something to this cross-country pastime after all. I got a little daring, deliberately going for hills instead of around them, keeping my knees bent to get down without flailing like a discarded marionette. At one point, the path turned and I found myself deep in the woods, underneath old and towering evergreens that almost blocked out the sunlight, and a sensation of mystery glowed through me. And the air! When you're inside all the time, it's easy to forget how fresh and crunchy the winter air can be.

This transformation to contentment had taken just a little time, and I almost forgot and forgave the beginning of my day. I skied and skied, as fast as I could and as slow as I wanted. I tumbled again and it was no crisis. I pretended to be an Olympic racer. I stopped for breath and looked around at the awesome winter world.

Then I heard them. Even after ditching me, even when I had found a few minutes of fun in the woods, Marco and Kelly were having more fun. I knew it was them even though I couldn't see them—puffs of steam rose from the other side of an uprooted tree bottom, and there was moaning. I stood still in my tracks because if I started up again, they would know I had heard them. Maybe there would be a scene. Or I could just continue on and pretend I hadn't heard, but then they'd probably think I was a nasty little Peeping Tom and they would retaliate in some way.

Marco must have brought a blanket or something in the backpack. Knowing him, I'd bet he'd probably brought an inflatable queen-size bed. Why go without just because you're in the woods? There were no words, just noises. As dead curious as I was about seeing this sex thing between a boy and a girl for real, I decided to go on as quietly as I could and not even look in their direction. The path bent around and the audio got better. I really wanted to look, because this might be as close as I ever got to the real thing. I felt stupid for being so completely intrigued, but for the first time I also understood that no matter how beautiful people are, they sound pretty ridiculous having sex. There wasn't a lot of difference between those romance noises and the grunts of someone on the pot having a hard time. I managed to fight my curiosity and look ahead, though it took some effort pretending to be engrossed in skiing.

"Oh, my God, oh, my God," one of them said and then "Jesus Christ," but they were such hoarse whispers that I couldn't make out who was praying to whom. Finally I was around another bend in the trail. They would have to be faced later, but I had gotten out of having to deal with them with their pants down. I couldn't imagine what I would have said if they had caught me catching them.

I skied for a long time, trying to sort out the jumble in my head. There was excitement, no doubt about that. I had heard two people having sex in distinct tones. My parents had always been up front about sex between a man and a woman, same-sex sex, AIDS, and condoms. I could probably recite the information back to them word for word. The script was technical and boring, always using words like *insert* and *deposit* that could be describing a pay phone. Sex was only exciting when it wasn't a lesson plan. I had seen some pornography—with Marco, who called *Penthouse "Pantyhose."*

Sex in the great outdoors was much more interesting than porn. Sex was what teenagers whose bodies actually changed did if they wanted. This was also one more example of how slippery the path out of babyhood was. While some kids my age were dating and going all the way, the closest I came to it was listening to other people and pretending I wasn't. From the sounds of it, Marco knew exactly what to do with a girl, whereas I was going home to some food, hot chocolate, and a nap.

Another hour had passed by the time I found my way back to the parking lot. Marco's Accord wasn't there anymore.

I wasn't all that surprised. I was a tagalong on this trip, nothing more; Marco and I would never hang out together again, just the two of us. There was something soothing about the realization, something calming about accepting the truth rather than trying to change it. Besides, I had discovered cross-country skiing and it didn't even bother me that I might have to devise some other plan to get home.

So I almost cheerfully took my skis off and, putting them awkwardly over my right shoulder, started walking home. When I was younger it was no big deal riding a bike a mere three miles, so walking it couldn't be that much worse. Anyone could do it. The air was still and fresh and the landscape beautiful.

Who knows how far I had gotten when my euphoria exploded like a piñata full of live grenades. I had been hot and sweaty under my clothes while I was skiing, and now I started to freeze. My skis wouldn't stay in place over my shoulder, inching slow and steady toward the ground until I dropped both of them. Also, my determination to wear these jeans finally backfired, because despite being thirsty like a desert dog, I had to pee really bad. My bladder was a hot-water bottle pressing on my abdomen and penis. If I somehow managed to get the pants unzipped I might find relief, but I'd be left with my fly wide open for the world. With my luck the button would pop, too, and I'd be carrying skis over my shoulder with my pants down around my ankles. I wasn't going to survive this day.

A car pulled up next to me. It was an older couple, old like grandparents, and they were driving their giant, white Oldsmobile. The window rolled down on the woman's side.

"Is everything okay, son?" the old guy asked from the driver's seat.

"Yeah, I'm okay."

"Tristan? Is that you? Do you remember me, Mrs. Schroeder?" It was my old fifth-grade teacher who had retired at the end of that year. The man must have been her husband.

"Hi," I said.

"I almost didn't recognize you. You've grown."

This was a trap. A fat kid grows antennae around adults. Very early on I learned to read signals that would help me steer grown-ups away from the tubby subject. Once I was collecting for UNICEF all by myself up and down our street, and some older lady had tried to trap me. After giving me some coins for my can, she had said, "You're such a handsome boy." Now to the untrained ear this would sound like a compliment, definitely no cause for alarm. But except for Mom and Dad, no one ever told me I was handsome without qualifying it. "You know," she had continued, innocent-like, "my grandmother was heavy. She was such a pretty woman, too, but she just couldn't keep the weight off and she wound up dying of the hardening of the arteries." I had her right: A long lecture was coming from this woman whose teeth were so brown from smoking they might have been varnished.

So even though Mrs. Schroeder could save me from the thirst and the exhaustion and the cold and the loss of bladder control, I had to think quickly and get rid of her.

"Nice car," I said.

She looked confused. "Oh. Well, yes. Would you like a ride to town?"

To turn down the offer was stupid, possibly deadly. So of course I said, "No, thanks," and tried to smile. "I'm waiting for my friends."

"Do your friends know you're zigzagging along the side of the highway?"

I laughed, a dry, dusty laugh. "No, it's okay. I just wanted to get a head start."

They both looked at me like I was probably now in the special school.

"Are you sure?"

"Yeah. Thanks."

Mrs. Schroeder pulled out her cell phone. "Do you want to call someone to pick you up?"

"No, no, that's okay. Thanks."

"Well, all right," she said. "You're sure?"

I nodded, which tipped some cold sweat droplets into my eyes.

The window rolled up and the old man pulled the car back onto the highway slowly.

That was the dumbest thing you've ever done, I thought. But I couldn't get in the car with two old people and have them drive me home like a little kid who's lost his mommy.

An idea brought hope rebounding. Why didn't I think of that before, I almost said aloud. I moved off the highway shoulder and placed the uncooperative skis on the snow. Make them do the work, I thought. Don't carry them. Great idea, except I hadn't gotten any more adept at getting into the bindings, and the land slanted downhill from the pavement. So, when I had one foot in a catch after a long struggle, I'd lose the other ski down the grade. Or I'd fall sideways. Then I thought to go down the embankment to even terrain and put the skis on there. But the farther I went down, the deeper the snow got, until I couldn't see my foot or the ski I was trying to latch. Climbing back to the side of the road, I was hot, cold, out of breath, encased in snow, and once again trying to carry my ornery skis. For a second I considered throwing them onto the highway, to teach them a lesson. Instead, I took up my impossible trudging.

Just when I was sure I was done for, that I might as well have been alone in the Yukon, an SUV slowed down and pulled over. My father was driving the giant car he had bought to make him feel less old about being with Cyndi.

"What are you doing walking along the road, Tri? Get in."

I was so relieved to see him that I didn't even think about all the lies I would need to tell to protect the guilty.

"Dad, I need a soda. I'm so thirsty."

"Let's go." Everything was okay. Then he insisted on knowing the story.

"It's nothing," I said. "Just a day at the park."

"Out with it."

I didn't have the energy to invent, so I edited, left out details. I told him that Kelly and Marco were too fast for me, that I had gotten impatient waiting for them to come back for me, and left on my own.

He got angry. He always got this sort of dead look on his face when he was about to explode at Mom, like all expression had drained out with the color. He never yelled at me, so I knew he was ready to kill her over this.

"Dad," I said, when we stopped for a soda, "if

you tell Mom, she's going to flip at Kelly and I'm gonna pay when I get back to school. Besides," I said, feeling a jab of sorrow, "Marco's my friend."

"This is complete crap," he said, huffing and grimacing like he was trying not to blow. "They brought you there, they should have brought you home. You're soaking wet. I'm tempted to go over to his house and kick that boy's privileged ass myself."

"Yeah, that would improve things."

"I'm taking you back *home.* To *my* house. Get your soda." He sounded final. I trotted to the rest room where I shimmied my pants down without unzipping them and took one of the most gratifying pees ever. I got a grape soda and bottle of water from the rows of coolers. Dad paid for them and I sucked them down in the car.

"Dad," I said, between belches. "It's okay. Don't take me home. Take me to Mom's or else she's gonna be suspicious, and then she'll fight with Kelly and I'll have to go live in an abandoned car."

"So, in other words, this Kelly treats you like a dog, leaves you for dead, and you have to protect her?"

"It's called love." He looked annoyed and puzzled, then smiled.

"You're too quick, Tri."

"At some things."

"Marco Cavi is a jerk. And Kelly needs to shuffle back to Buffalo soon. I can't imagine your mother exactly getting on well with her."

"Nope, but there haven't been any fistfights yet. I'm waiting for Kelly to tell her she needs to lose a few pounds. I mean, what can I do to protect her then? Mom'll eat her alive."

"The sooner the better."

Dad stopped at the end of Frank's long driveway. No one would see me coming home without my guardians. I'd think up something to say when I got to the house.

"I don't like this," Dad said as he took out my skis and poles. "I don't like this cloak-and-dagger thing a bit."

"I'm okay. Someday we'll look back at this and laugh."

"Yuk yuk," he said, and gave me a hug. "Need money?"

"Yeah, why not?" He gave me ten dollars and another hug.

"Are you sure you don't want to come home with me? Just say the word and I'll go up there and holler at your mother until I actually feel something pop in my spine. It'll be just like it used to be."

"Now I see why you two fell in love in the first place."

We had taken too long with our good-byes. Frank was heading down the driveway in his small, sporty coupe slightly listing to the driver's side. He stopped, opened the window.

"Hey, Gordon," he said, looking confused and huge inside the tiny car. Then he frowned. "Tristan, where's Kelly?"

Caught red-handed, I couldn't say anything.

"What's going on?" Frank asked, almost a threat.

I said, "Dad picked me up."

"Why?" he asked, growing more excited. "Why didn't Marco drive you home?"

I was tempted to say he had frostbite on his southern cheeks, but instead settled for the lesser truth. "I couldn't find them. I got lost on the trail and couldn't find them again, so I just started home."

This was bad, my father and my almost step-father face-to-face, things not pleasant.

"Frank, I saw Tristan walking along Route 385 carrying skis," Dad said. He was trying to speak in measured tones and it wasn't working. "Evidently Kelly and that idiot Marco left him at the park."

"Where does he live, Tristan?" Frank asked like a judge in a death sentence kind of mood.

Dad looked at me, bit his lip. I didn't answer.

"Never mind," said Frank. "I'll find them myself." He sped off.

"I hope he doesn't," I said.

"The man has a right to know where his daughter is." Dad looked toward the house, a glimmer in his eyes.

"Oh no you don't," I said.

"Please? Just one little shouting match?"

"Go home."

His shoulders dropped a little. He waved and left.

So—except for the thirst and the full bladder and the death march along the highway and my mother's boyfriend going to capture two of the most popular kids in school because of me—nothing could ruin this day.

I told Mom the same half story I'd told Dad, but only after I put the equipment away and had something to eat.

By then Frank was driving up with Kelly. I ran into the family room and turned on the TV like I had been there for a while. Kelly sizzled in, and as she burned a trail to her room, she detoured over to me and whispered, "I wouldn't expect anything more from a little boy."

When she had slammed her bedroom door, Frank ambled in and sat down on the couch. "She's calling her mother," he said absently. "Suddenly the world looks rosy in Buffalo." That's all I heard, because I got up to go to my own room.

At first I was determined to escape to my father's, but that might make things worse, like I had something to hide. Then a better idea came to me. After I had a chance to get warm and dry I would take those skis out for a little spin on Frank's property. That would work off some of the fear, and I wouldn't need a ride home. I would soon need to get out of this house, switch schools, possibly assume a new identity. But for now I was going to ski.

Later, Mom filled me in on the gruesome details. Kelly and Marco were not in the hot tub when Frank arrived because of the Cavis' crippling misfortune of a broken filter. But they were out of breath and their clothes and hair were crazy when they finally answered the door after Frank rang and pounded over and over. Marco's parents were not home because they were never home, and they probably didn't want to interfere with Marco's personal life anyway. Kelly had been so caught off guard that she couldn't think of any instant stories, and Frank had told Marco in that annoying, protective, old-man way that fathers have, "You are no longer welcome in my house, young man."

I was dead.

Chapter 12

I spent the next week at Dad's, but had such a bad cold that I missed three days of school. That was good because I had broken the Montreal bond and didn't know what to expect.

That next Monday I made it through school, catching only glimpses of Marco and Kelly from a distance. At the end of the day I went home to Frank's house, where Kelly gave me a stiff "Hi." I went straight to my room as if she'd sent me.

About half an hour before Mom was supposed to come home, I heard clamoring in the house. It was Marco and he was getting ready to go. Evidently Kelly knew just when to smuggle him in and out.

I waited until I heard the kitchen door open and knew they had gone outside. I went to the kitchen for some water. They were on the back deck talking. I should have headed right back to safety, but I was intrigued by their defiance and I wanted to eavesdrop. If I had to be on the outside of society, at least I could listen in on its conversations. Big mistake.

At first I heard mumbling, then a little muffled laughter, then nothing. They must have been kissing good-bye. Then some more laughter and Marco's deep voice. This kind of interaction was so foreign to me that they might as well have been from a different planet, never mind a different caste. I had the faucet on at a trickle in case I got caught. Then they took a break from kissing, because they were talking plenty now.

"How much do you think he weighs?" Marco asked. They must have been analyzing Frank, Kelly's favorite disappointment.

"Two hundred?"

"Really?" he said shocked. "I didn't think it was that much."

I was shocked, too. Frank must have weighed more than two hundred.

"No, couldn't be. I forbid it." Marco was good at echoing sophistication. Then he added, "No one weighs that much at his age." He laughed.

"You're right. That's too much. He's just a little round. Maybe he'll grow out of it soon."

"I hope so. He's always had a problem with it."

"He looks like he's lost some. He's been playing in the woods."

"Yeah, he needs to get into shape bad."

"I guess he's trying," she said. "I've been there, and it's not like snapping your fingers."

"He could have a cardio arrest someday."

"Well he's got a really bad role model in this house."

Then there was silence punctuated only by purring. They were back to kissing, while I stood waiting for my cardio arrest. It seemed possible at that moment.

"Him in the attic still weirds me out," Marco said. "*What* was he doing with that monk's uniform on?"

"I don't know. But really it was my father's fault. He probably built the cheapest house he could."

"You have to admit it's a little strange."

"He's okay," Kelly said. "He's still a boy. I just wish he could keep his mouth closed once in a while."

It was something other than heart failure. Instead, it was a feeling that didn't happen to me often. I'd never had much of a temper, but now I could feel something hot and urine-like bubbling under my skin. It was suicide to stop this, but it had to be stopped. My best friend was no longer my best friend and now he was discussing me like I was some perverted kid who lived in the apartment next door. This anger was either a source of strength or self-destruction. It didn't matter because it felt right. It was terrible and heavy at the same time, but for once I was mad instead of injured. I had to let them know I hadn't said a word about their wrestling match in the woods.

Then Marco dropped another bomb, the second one in two minutes.

"Don't forget to come early and help me set up for the party."

Party?

"I'll be there around seven," she said.

"How are you going to get around your dad?"

"I'll fix it. Don't worry."

Marco had never actually invited me to his parties before. I was just expected to be there. Now I was expected *not* to be there.

Dazed, I started walking out of the kitchen. Kelly bounced in and my anger bounced back. Suddenly I turned to her and said, "By the way, I was looking for something for my father. In the attic that day."

"I don't care what you were doing," she said, smooth as a beach ball.

"I heard Marco ask."

She took a menacing step closer to me. She pointed in my face. "What my boyfriend says to me is my business." She looked as big and scary as a state trooper at that moment. Still I felt driven by a reckless defiance.

"I heard you guys."

"Heard what?" she asked, like it was nothing.

"About how much I weigh and stuff."

She smiled. I expected more indifference. Instead she sliced me open. "Is that what you were doing when you came flying into my bedroom? With your trick-or-treat costume on? Trying to hear what grown-ups say to each other?"

"Huh?"

"Why don't you try to be a little more mature? And get some friends of your own and talk to them?"

I could barely get out a "What?"

"You heard me. Is *that* what you're about? Telling on people like a spoiled little brat?"

I stood there, almost breathing. She couldn't have been more terrifying if she had a gun.

"I never said anything about anything."

"Grow up, Tristan."

"I didn't. I swear. I never said a word. But I had to get home. I thought you guys had left me."

"You're too old to be such a child." She started walking away.

"At least I get along with my father."

She turned back to me, beautiful and bloodthirsty. "What did you say?"

"Why don't you leave Frank alone?" I said. It was more of a whisper than a question, the fear soaking up the sound.

"What did you say?"

My voice trembled like I was challenging a giant lizard. "Oh, forget it."

She slapped me right across the face. It didn't matter how hard, because the fact that she had done it staggered me. I stepped back a few feet. Tears stung my eyes. My heart pumped like it could beat its way out of my chest. Just as my whole body veered completely out of its lane, Kelly's expression softened. She smiled, then gave a little laugh.

"Oh, Tristan, you really are just a boy. But that's okay. It's like you're a little brother. You'll be all right." She patted me on the shoulder. Then, as if to prove her point, tears toppled over my eye rims and my mommy walked in.

"What's going on here?"

I was about to tell her to go away, but Kelly beat me to the spin.

"Tristan and I were just . . ." I turned around and walked as fast as I could out of that kitchen, so no one would see how I ran.

Mom followed me, and from the sounds of it, Kelly was fast on her heels. I slammed my bedroom door shut and jumped on the bed, but Mom let herself right in, shutting the door on Kelly. Kelly opened it and started coming in.

"Not now, Kelly," Mom said. She even scared me.

Kelly paused, then said, "Sure," as if it were her idea, and left.

"Tristan, what's wrong?"

I couldn't talk with the cramping in my throat, but I managed to squawk out, "Just leave me alone." Instead she came over and tried to hug me, but I turned to the wall. Crying like a big fat baby at my age was what someone like me would do. I might as well act the part.

"Go, Ma, I mean it."

"I'm not leaving. I'll wait." She sat at my desk

without a word while I choked and gasped and did everything possible not to cry. I knew the beast was just outside the door, and I knew Mom was looking for a good reason to fight her.

When the worst of the wracking had drained away, I sat up on my bed, moist.

"I want the truth," Mom said in her usual pushy-decisive way.

"I'm fifteen years old and my mother's still coming to my rescue. That's the truth."

"Well," she said a little more gently, "seeing as you'll still be borrowing money from me when you're forty, I guess it's okay for you to let me come to your rescue at fifteen. Do you want to talk about it?"

"No."

"Tri, I know when something's wrong."

"Brilliant."

"What is it?"

"Nothing."

"Which means it's something."

There was a rapid knock. Kelly opened the door again. Mom stood up.

"Anne, this is no big deal. I think you—"

"Kelly, you've got the rest of the house. We

need a quiet moment." Kelly stared her down for a few seconds and Mom stared back. I expected them to start circling each other, followed by some growling and snapping, but Kelly backed down. She shut the door again, with a little clap this time. This is what chaos looks like, I thought.

"Tri," Mom said.

"No, Ma, I just want you to leave me alone. I want everybody to leave me alone."

"But I want to know—"

"Mom, forget it. I'm just . . . I don't want to go over it again."

"It's Kelly," Mom said. "I don't know what I'm going to do. I have no patience for her at all. And I don't like whatever game it is she's playing with you."

"She's not doing anything. She's just part of a different world."

All of a sudden Mom looked weak, pained. She sat down again, turned her head away from me. "I don't know, Tri. I just don't know. I don't hurry into things generally, so I still can't figure out how I got myself into all this."

"This what?"

"This household!" she shouted as if it were

obvious. Then she said, quieter, "You don't divorce your husband one year and move into another tangled situation the next."

"You and Frank are happy."

"Yeah. Delirious. I got involved with a man without knowing anything about his child. Who's the idiot?"

"You're supposed to be comforting me," I said. Then I regretted it, because I could see how miserable she was. There was a long pause. She turned.

"If you want to talk . . ." she started.

"No. I just want to be alone."

She shook her head and snarled a laugh. "There's some frosting in the cupboards somewhere. Maybe I'll eat it right out of the can in front of Kelly."

"Well, I just got a good report card from her. She told Marco I was losing weight. Just not enough."

Suspicion quivered across her face. "Where did she see Marco?"

"At school," I lied. "I mean on the phone."

"Was he here?"

"No."

"Ah, what difference does it make? I wouldn't be surprised if Marco was living in the attic. No one can control them."

"What do you mean the attic?" I asked, alarmed.

"It's a joke, Tri."

"Oh, right, well, Marco would never settle for the attic anyway. He needs a whole room for his clothes."

"He's one of a kind. That's the nicest thing I can say about him."

"Look, Ma, don't ask me to betray the secret honor code of teenagers, even if I don't look like one yet."

"Just remember. Don't let problems get huge. If you need me, ask me. It's just like the drunken driving contract we have. If you find yourself at a party with no ride home except with—"

"The first problem is finding a party to get drunk at," I said.

"Well, when you do, you can always call—"

"Yeah, I know," I said. "I'm tempted to call you from Dad's at 3:00 A.M. just to see if you really mean it."

"I really mean it. Just don't expect good hair at that hour." She looked in the mirror. "Or any hour, for that matter." She leaned over and kissed me. When she turned for the door, she straightened her shoulders like she was heading for battle, and left my room.

Chapter 13

It was the day before Midwinter Break and that night the party would happen. Despite all good reasoning, I could not deal with that party. I wouldn't necessarily have gone, but I still wanted to have been invited.

Parties. It sounded like everyone in school was going to Marco's house, except me and anyone associated with band. I couldn't concentrate half the time thinking about why it would be so hard for him to invite one more person. Of course, that one person was me, and that was why.

Friday started out bad and inched toward worse all day. The paper we had been assigned for European studies was almost due. My uncool fascination with the English Reformation had an advantage in that my parents bought me any book I wanted. I had written a meticulous paper on the Tower of London. I had this persistent hope that maybe if I talked to Marco about needing help with his, he would mention that he was having a party. But after all that had happened, there was ice between us now. So why did I try bringing the topic up before class?

"How's your research paper coming?" I asked him as we were walking in. "Need me to read what you've got so far?" If he heard me, he pretended not to.

"Need any help—"

"What are you, my mother?" he asked smoothly as if he wanted an answer. It was loud enough for more than just the two of us to hear. "You're not my mother, dude. And she's got a deeper voice." He winked a sinister wink.

I looked at him, waiting for my vocal cords to be handed back.

"It's all under control. I've got it all under control, kid," he said, sitting down. I made sure to find a seat nowhere near him.

I couldn't concentrate the entire class, although this was my favorite subject of all. Mrs. Junker had hooked me at the beginning of the school year with the fall of the Roman Empire and the beginning of the Dark Ages. I usually took really detailed notes, but today I sat in class, stung. Marco's words ran through my head with cleats. I kept replaying the evidence over and over, trying to think of a way to convince him that I hadn't squealed on them, that I had definitely not told Frank the sizzling-snow detail, and that the truth was I had been caught trying to protect them. When I would come back to the present and realize I had not taken any notes at all, I would start writing something down, then drift back to my imaginary defense.

That was only the introductory paragraph of my day. Next there was the Tim Boggs incident. The whole world wanted to bite off a piece of me. One of the benefits of being in band was getting out of class for a lesson every sixth day of the rotating schedule. I headed toward the rehearsal room. Walking through the science wing, I saw Tim Boggs sitting with a bunch of guys on the windowsill overlooking the courtyard, waiting for their teacher to show up. This was a dangerous setup. No one else was in the hall, and that meant I had to walk conspicuously by a bunch of kids who had nothing but me to comment on. It didn't matter if they knew me or not. Unless they somehow didn't see me, they would be obliged to say something as I walked by. Seeing Tim Boggs there, I thought I might be safe, because we had once been friends. I had saved him during the Iroquois unit in seventh grade when he was supposed to bring in half the corn muffins for our presentations and he forgot, and I brought in enough so that nobody noticed his mistake. Also, since he now had the reputation of being constantly stoned, I figured he was too relaxed to make fun of me.

I approached this cluster of people—Mike Black, Steve LaFontaine, Greg Fantauzzi, maybe more—all kids who I didn't know too well but didn't have a good feeling about. They were athletes, tall and big, with raucous, deep voices, too. They would no doubt be at Marco's party. Was I supposed to look at them, say hi, maybe, or ignore them and act like I was deep in thought? I was too afraid to make a firm decision, so I glanced over and sort of nodded my head to the now silent pack. I jerked my head back so I could stare straight ahead. There was a snicker, then Tim Boggs's nasally voice as only it could be, "Hey, Tristan, man, if you're gonna have big tits, you need to wear a bra." They laughed with triumph, and someone whistled, and someone made another joke I didn't quite hear, but which caused more explosive laughing. Then they broke into conversation again, forgetting me. I kept walking with my pitiful I'm-a-good-sport smile, even though I could feel poison shooting through my limbs and throbbing to dead ends in my fingers and toes.

There was more. Gym had changed for me, too, this year, or better yet I had changed toward it. I had always in the past signed up for the first module—the active one where you ran a lot and played like you meant it, things like flag football and tennis and even jogging. Yet by the end of my freshman year, I started signing up for the modified ones, the mods that attracted the lumpy or uncoordinated or just plain scared kids. This quarter I was in the archery mod, an idle and useless activity if there ever was one. I spent most of the time sitting, waiting while someone else took a few bad shots at the target. Then I'd pick up the bow, be surprised at how hard it was to handle, try not to show it, and pretend I didn't care that the arrow hit the bleachers each time.

But you couldn't get out of the yearly fitness test, no matter which lazy mod you took. Our pre-Midwinter Break present was that regular gym was canceled and we all met in one huge bunch. We got tested and then would be given a score to prove how fit we weren't. We'd had the same test in middle school, too, but then it had been fun. I had looked forward to it then because it had been a challenge to do as many sit-ups as possible in thirty seconds or to get as many agility thrusts in before the whistle blew. In ninth grade, however, the fitness test had become a lot harder than I'd remembered. And this year my body was proving downright uncooperative. Plus there were so many more people in gym class, and of different ages, that it was like being in the military.

Will Zumigata took me under his wing, acting as my sit-up partner because no one more intensely evil was available. He encouraged me this way throughout the entire test: "Come on, Dough Boy. One more, butterball. You can do it, Humpty." He probably did get a few more out of me than I would have on my own, but it cemented my paranoia about physical fitness testing. Instead of competing against my own previous record, now I was fighting not to perform the way a fat kid did. I not only dragged my extra pounds but the pulsing torment of believing every eye was on me as I ran sprints around the cones at both ends of the gym. It was grim good luck that Bart Phillips, a senior, was in the lane next to me during my sprints. He was the slowest kid in school, wide and old-mannish and an easy target. While I ran as if my life depended on it, and tried not to gasp for air, Bart waddled down the court a lap slower than me. There was no way any gym teacher could have protected him from the hooting and howling. Marco, on the other hand, flew down the court as natural as walking.

After class, Will walked by my gym locker and called clear and strong, "How's it going, Dough-eeee?" He was about seven feet tall and he stood at the end of the row where my locker was and put his giant foot up on the bench.

"What size do you wear?"

I kept putting my clothes on, shaking a little, hoping I was asleep.

"Well, what size?" He was not going away without an answer.

"I don't know," I mumbled.

"Pretty big for that little jockstrap, Dough Boy, aren't you? You need a bigger one. You don't want to crush them things down there." He smiled like giving this kind of advice was a good deed.

Paralyzed as my head was, my body kept automatically doing what it was doing.

"Listen, butterball, you need to take two gym classes a day. I'm worried about ya."

I considered crawling into the locker, but then

figured I would probably get stuck halfway in and someday a monument would be built on my backside.

Finally dressed, I knew he wasn't going to let me go without a payoff. I tried to look casual as I made my way, but he stuck his huge, long leg across my path, his foot up against the lockers.

"Aw, come on. Don't be such a girl," he said. "I'm just teasing." Then he wrapped his giant tentacle around my neck, pulling me down, a demon big brother.

"What's the password?" he asked, tightening his arm.

"I don't know," I said, in a giveaway weak voice.

One of the gym teachers, Mr. Clark, walked by just then.

"Come on, Zumigata. You and your little buddy get out of here and get to class."

"Just having a little fun with my little friend, Dough Boy," Will said.

"Dough Boy?" asked Mr. Clark with a smile. "Listen, Zumi, one day that Dough Boy is going to be taller and wider than you and kick your ass. And I hope he does."

Will gave me an affectionate shove that almost

knocked me over. Righting myself, I got out of there fast before there were any more attacks of brotherly love.

That was two fat things in one morning and one comment about my voice, and that should have been it for a long time. But how I thought things should go made no difference.

My French teacher, Madame Cannon, who must have been named after her mouth, continued the cycle. Most people were having trouble with conjugating imperative verbs because most people in the class had trouble paying attention to any aspect of the French language, so she was reviewing a bunch of them. "This is something you should have learned in eighth grade," she said, and clapped her hands. "We're deeply into sophisticated tenses. That's what tenth graders across the state are doing. Here we are backing up to beginning French. What did they teach you?" She seemed to have forgotten that she had also been our eighth-grade teacher.

With this small outburst completed, she ran through a standard list of French commands, pointing at people for effect. "*Mange!* Eat! *Regarde!* Watch! *Chante!* Sing! *Engraisse!* Gain weight!" Then she pointed at me, "*Maigris!* Lose weight!"

She looked stricken at first, and she should have, because I was one of her only allies, one kid who didn't constantly morph pronunciation of French words into obscene English. Marco was especially talented this way, for example, taking the French word *piscine* and emphasizing the *piss*. There were worse ones, usually about body parts, which he never got tired of.

And now, on one of the worst days I could shoulder, she showed her gratitude by turning on me. Accidentally, maybe, but those Freudian slips can't be discounted.

"*Maigris!* Lose weight!"

Some people giggled at this latest insult, but most of the class didn't get it because they weren't paying attention. I refused to look at Marco, although I was pretty sure I heard his exaggerated laugh.

"*Continuons.* Let's continue," she said with a slight quiver. My face glowed like an embarrassment thermometer. The world was a huge and unmanageable place, and I wasn't sure I was a match for it.

That was three fat things. But Friday wasn't finished with me yet. When I was leaving school for the day and practically on the bus, I realized my math book was still in my locker. This was no small concern seeing as it would mean there would be no crowd of bodies in the hallways and I might have to pass by small, pernicious groups of kids. I went back to get the book, and since I managed to escape any persecution to, at, and from my locker, I thought I had gotten away with something. Instead, by the time I got back outside, I had missed the bus. In the past I could have gotten a ride with Marco. He used to not mind if I rode home with him once in a while, if I didn't abuse the privilege. Now that was not an option, so I was going to have to walk four miles to the village. I could have called one of my homes, but I knew Dad, Cyndi, and Mom were at work that early in the afternoon. I didn't have Frank's number at his studio, and if I called his house I would get Kelly, who would be entertaining Marco. Neither of them ever bothered with ninth period. It was impossible to ask her to get Frank, and then ask him to give me a ride to my father's. So I had to walk, and it was winter.

Who should pull up next to me as I made my way down the hill from the high school but my old pal Will Zumigata? Twice in one day. It was like he had a tracking device. Maybe I really *was* his best friend and no one had informed me. Some other guy I didn't know was driving and already laughing at something.

"Hey, big guy," Will called with a chuckle. "Want a ride?" I ignored him, hoping for a fire truck to scare him off, or maybe a SWAT team.

"I'm talking to you, Dough Boy. You deaf or you just rude?" His friend laughed like a drunken cowboy. They pulled over close to the curb but kept driving. I knew I should run, blind as it may have been, rather than keep going as if nothing was wrong, because I certainly wasn't fooling them. The cowboy drove slowly. This could go on for miles, and if it were some test of my endurance, I was going to need a remedial class.

"Ahhhhh, wanna potty toooo-night," Will sang in a shout. Then he asked, "What about you, Dough Boy? Wanna party?"

"Party!" the other one yelled past Will.

This kind of thing went on for hours, at least that's how two minutes felt. The worst thing was my concern about appearances. No matter how scared or nauseated I was that they would never stop, I didn't want to look embarrassed or afraid. Every step I took was a marvel of acting.

"Jesus, Dough Boy, you look like you're going to have a stroke. Do you want a ride or not?"

"Uh, no, that's okay."

"You sure? I don't want to read in the paper about the Dough Boy dropping dead. His little dough heart just stopping and his little white body turning blue. I'd feel guilty."

"No," I said. "I live real close."

"Don't walk on the lake whatever you do. You don't want to be falling through the ice like you did with that ceiling. The Dough Boy could drown that way. Little frozen Dough Boy."

Some involuntary reaction of mine to this dart must have concerned him.

"Stop," he said to the cowboy. The car jerked to a standstill. "Dough Boy, seriously, are you gonna be all right?"

I couldn't answer.

"You look like you're sick. Was it the gym test? Too much for you? Just get in. Where are you going?"

I shook my head, not stopping.

With that, my best friend's patience ran out.

"Okay, see ya, Humpty."

They pulled away, speeding up. The cowboy honked the horn a few times, and they were gone. I hurried home as fast as I could, no time to think. I didn't feel like crying or fainting, and I wasn't even angry. I just wanted to get home. A home with no Kelly.

Chapter 14

By the time I got to the village, I was freezing and hot at the same time, just like when I had been abandoned with my skis. And starving. Dad was not home yet. I let myself in, but I really needed someone to talk to, even if I refused to divulge a single detail about my day or complain that Marco's party was tonight. I half expected Will Zumigata to be in the kitchen when I got there with the oven preheated, holding a cookie sheet.

The good thing about imagining your worst fears is that you can only stand the thoughts for so long, and then numbness takes over. By the time Dad got home, the immediate past was so big and burdensome that it seemed unreal and I didn't want to talk it over. I went about things as usual, did my homework with only some distraction, and watched TV with Dad and Cyndi, who came by after dinner. Kids were probably just starting to show up at Marco's about now, and here I was getting sleepy. Oh, well, I thought, if I were there, I'd just stand around with a beer that I couldn't drink. I'd have to make it look like I didn't mind the screaming music, too.

Dad said good night to me when I finally resigned myself to another early one, and that's when I asked him: "So, what if I came to live here full-time? Would that break you and Cyndi up?"

He sat down on my bed, a quizzical look on his face. "What's going on now, Tri?"

"Nothing."

"And what kind of question is that to ask me if my son would break up my relationship?"

"Nothing. Just wondering."

"I can tell when something's wrong. Is it still that Kelly?"

"Yeah, it's that Kelly. I'm sick of her. Her and Marco."

"Do they give you a hard time? At school? Because I can't imagine Frank letting Marco in his house again."

"No," I said. "It's just that . . . I can't explain it. It's like I'm the family pet or something."

"That Kelly's a piece of work."

"Yeah, a piece of something."

"I'll talk to your mother."

"No, Dad."

"I will. It will be okay."

"If you talk to Mom, it's going to filter back to Kelly, and then she's going to take it out on me. She's like the queen of the school now."

"What do you mean take it out on you? What's going on?"

"Nothing. Nothing. It's not just them. You know what I mean."

"No, I don't think I do. What is it, then?"

"It would be like being a tattletale or something, and you know how that is. I just want a change. And Frank—"

"What, is Frank on your case, too?" He sounded annoyed now and faintly worried.

"No, not exactly. But he and Mom are always at each other's throats, and he's always on edge."

"You need to stay here, then. Done."

I should have been relieved and grateful for him saying yes so quickly, but I had this suspicion that it had something to do with trumping Mom. I knew from remarks Dad made under his breath that there was some residual tension between them over the cross-country day stuff. He didn't exactly blame her for it but insinuated that she was exposing me to emotional viruses by making me live in a crazy house. But maybe Kelly was right. Maybe I needed to grow up a little. Still, I couldn't help wondering aloud.

"What about Cyndi?"

"What about Cyndi? She knows where you stand with me. Besides, you live here every other week as it is."

"Are you sure? I mean, Mom and Frank were happy before Kelly came along, and now I don't even remember what it was like before her."

"So you're comparing yourself to Kelly?"

"Yeah, I thought I'd try to get you two in shape."

"We're in shape, Cyndi and I. A variety of shapes."

"Good, because I'm going to make tofu Easter bunnies this year."

"It'll be fine," he said, though I detected uncertainty. "It'll be fine."

"I need to talk to Mom. It won't be easy."

"That was always my experience with her."

"Dad," I said. "Don't."

"I know. I'm sorry. But you're right. She's going to ask a lot of questions."

"Yeah, and I'm going to have to try to keep her from gnawing Kelly's door down afterward."

"Well, I have to admit I was always proud of your mother's . . . um . . . spirit. Tell me something: This Kelly. Doesn't her mother want her back yet? Isn't it her turn to mind the little darling?" I thought of Kelly sitting on my bed at Frank's house, beautiful and radiating confidence and perfume, then shouting at her mother over the phone like her words were compressed air she couldn't hold back.

"I guess. Anyway, I'm tired. Good night, Dad."

"Night, Tri."

He left. I lay there wondering how I was going to manage the rest of the school year, never mind the rest of my high-school career. My social star was really high in the sky. My former friend was having a party the whole school was probably going to, and all I had was a reputation for falling through floors and blabbing on people. A reputation like that was certain death. I was going to have to do something, but I had no idea what, not even one bad idea to start with.

Then there was a knock at my door, and I said, "Come in." Cyndi popped her cute little head around the door and asked if it was okay for her to come all the way in.

"Sure," I said, sitting up.

She snuck into my room like she was afraid the reform-school matron would catch her. "Tri, first of all, of course you can stay here full-time. This is your home, not mine. Don't be silly."

"I thought if you were thinking of moving in—"

"I'll still think about it. You're not going to scare me off, believe me. The last guy I dated had a son who kept trying to sit on my lap."

"Oh. He needed a mother, I guess."

"He was eighteen."

"Ew."

"Anyway, everything's cool. Besides, I need someone closer to my own age around here."

I laughed but couldn't think of a smart reply. "Thanks."

She ventured a little closer to the bed. "Good night." Then she sneaked off, closing my door quietly as if I were already asleep.

I was welcome and safe here. Maybe icebergs would surface eventually, but unless Cyndi had a son or daughter she wasn't telling anyone about, I think I could handle most things that could happen at Dad's. I was completely alert by now, a surge of good feeling toward Cyndi and dread about Mom and Frank, and Marco's party rising up. I figured I would not be able to get to sleep at all that night.

But I woke up and it was Saturday morning, bright and promising because it was Kelly and Marco and school-free, and best of all ready to deliver a dayful of cross-country skiing. Once Dad had realized I liked the sport, he had a gush of divorced parent generosity and bought me cross-country skis and tossed in a pair of snowshoes as a bonus.

There was a clean coating of snow on the ground, not enough to get Dad irritated about the driveway, but enough to make the outside world look replenished and alive again. He, Cyndi, and I went skiing at the park, and I had the secret satisfaction of having to wait for them from time to time—especially Cyndi. I never fell either, although that's not necessarily a sign of a good skier, but I enjoyed being the one of the three of us who never floundered in the snow. We had such a good time that once in a while I forgot completely about all the things I was supposed to be worried about.

Each time I skied I understood something about freedom. This self-propelling over the snow in the midst of all the natural beauty really was in a way like skating through the woods, but impossible to do on skates. Something was happening to me, a new discovery, and one that made me feel not only awake again like when I was a young kid and went biking for hours, but attuned to a quieter world around me. As long as I didn't have to race anybody, I could become an addict.

After we were done, Dad took us to lunch at Derrick's, a café kind of place in the village. "Why don't you invite Peter to ski this week?" he asked. "Maybe tomorrow even. We can all go together again."

"What if his father wants to come?"

"Okay. The more the merrier."

"He looks like Henry VIII."

"Oh right, him."

Even though I didn't really want to go out on an excursion with a bunch of old people, I felt content. Since I was lighthearted for a change, I was unprepared for the next shot.

"What's that fat kid got? That looks good," I heard from another table. I couldn't actually see who said it, or any possible suspects, but it didn't matter. Right away I went into the robotlike state that happens when I'm under attack and don't know how to fight back. I ate some more of my lunch dispiritedly, trying to stay with the conversation, but only answering questions, not concentrating on what anyone—even myself—was saying. Instead I was wondering if I really had gained a lot of weight and just didn't know it, though my clothes fit the same. I didn't get out of breath any faster than usual. What was going on?

It took Dad and Cyndi awhile to notice, but by then it was time to go. In the car Dad asked me if something was wrong.

"No," I said.

"Well you got quiet in there all of a sudden," he said.

"I need a nap."

"Come on, Tri. Something's been bothering you since yesterday. Out with it. No secrets. No big ones anyway."

It flitted through my head that I should just tell him at least one of the things that was dragging on me, and I almost began talking about not being invited to the party. Then, abruptly, the impulse shrunk.

"Nothing. I hate being a teenager," I said.

"I hated being a teenager, too," Cyndi said. "I still hate that I ever was one."

She was quiet for a moment. Then added, "You know, I remember people always telling me when I was a teenager that I should be so happy to be young. That is, when they weren't telling me how pretty I'd be if I lost some weight. That's what an old person tells a young person, that youth is wonderful, but that's crazy. You've got to have lost your memory in a war to believe that."

Fortunately Dad didn't insist on a big gathering for skiing the next day. As much as I liked being with him, I thought that at some point I should be trying to establish some new friends to replace the old one. So it was just me and Peter and the park, and that was okay. Out there in the woods, parties didn't matter.

I had been having a fine time like I usually did on my skis, but it looked like there was no safe place.

"Is it true you caved in the ceiling in your mother's house?" he asked.

I didn't feel like answering. I felt like skiing off and leaving that topic in the trees. Instead I played along, hoping to rush things. "No. I didn't."

"I thought I heard about it somewhere."

"Nope, not me."

"Really?"

"Really." I figured it was okay to lie when the truth was no one's business.

"Yeah, well, Anthony and Gretchen didn't believe it either."

"How are things going with them?" I asked to derail him, then realized that once again I had no idea about these two people I ate lunch with every day.

"Okay, I think." He must have been bored with his investigation so he went on to the next annoying topic.

"My dad's on a new diet."

"What is it?"

"Cabbage soup."

"Cabbage soup?"

"Yeah."

"Isn't that what they torture prisoners of war with?"

"It works," he said. "You eat only cabbage soup for a week, and your body goes into a weight-loss mode that keeps going after the week's over."

"What if you don't make it through the week, say just a few days of cabbage soup? Or a few minutes?"

"No," he said defensively. "It's all or nothing. I'm going to try it, too."

"So how many days has your father done so far?"

"He's done the whole week. Now he's in day five of spiraling."

"What's spiraling?"

"That's what they call it when you just start losing weight and it doesn't stop no matter what you eat. The soup changes your body chemistry."

"So, you make it through a week and then you can eat a whole wedding cake and lose weight?"

"Yep."

"How much weight has he lost spiraling?"

"None. Yet."

We skied awhile in silence.

Chapter 15

The vacation fell on Dad's week, but Mom asked me to come visit her Wednesday because that was her day off. She took me to lunch and then we went back to Frank's house for a while. I should have escaped before dinner, but I idled too long, and before I knew it all four of us were sitting around the table. Maybe it was the angle I was seeing them at, but as my eyes ricocheted from face to face, each person looked different eating. Mom's features were washed out. Frank was an old man, older than the one I knew, graying and lined. Kelly, when she wasn't talking, looked like a little girl, especially when she was taking a drink of milk. Once again the grief of wanting my old family back burst through me.

Just when I couldn't chew another bite of my vegetarian lobster roll, Kelly broke my stupor. She had a happy announcement to make.

"Marco is taking me to the Queen of Hearts Dance at school on Valentine's Day. You are the best father in the world."

Mom blinked, almost audibly.

"Well," Kelly said, sounding a little paranoid now. "Don't you have something to say?"

None of us did.

"You always have something to say."

"Have a wondrous time," Mom said.

"Why so sarcastic?" Kelly asked.

"I said have a good time."

"Anne, why don't you just come out and say you don't like Marco?"

"He's sensational. I wish I had ten of him."

"There. That's sarcasm. Did you hear that?"

"Kelly . . . ," Frank said.

I looked down at my food as if I would discover gold there.

"He's not stupid," Kelly said in the tone she used to explain the obvious to a bunch of stupid people. "He's learning disabled."

"I would like to eat in peace," Frank said. Then he looked at Mom. "Are you mad at me for letting Kelly go to the dance with Marco? I thought maybe he's learned his lesson by now. He won't mess with me again."

"I'm sure he's learned a lesson, Frank, but not what you think."

"You don't know what you're talking about," Kelly said.

Mom put her napkin down, and twisted her lips. "Frank, maybe I should get an apartment."

There was a horrid silence. Then Frank, sounding like the jury had not seen it his way, said, "Because Marco's taking her—"

Mom laughed, a short, nasty grunt. "Marco doesn't have anything to do with it. You . . . Kelly and you need to work this thing out. Tristan and I are just in the way. And we're full of shrapnel all the time."

"Anne," Frank said, raising his voice. "This isn't fair."

"I'm sorry. I take full responsibility. Believe me, if I'd had any idea that things were going to be like this when we first got together, I would have asked every question I could. This is entirely my fault. But—and I do want to clarify that I'm not rambling—making a mistake does not mean suffering for it the rest of your life."

"It's because of me," Kelly said with a sneer. "I'll go live with my mother again. I won't disturb your happy little family." She started to get up.

"Kelly, sit down," Mom said, and Kelly actually did. "I'm taking the entire blame. Enjoy it while it lasts. But the objective truth is you fight a lot."

"The objective truth," Kelly said, and smirked.

"Yes. Objective. Anyone can see that you fight a lot. Anyone can hear it who doesn't live next to a cement plant. And it was very, very stupid of me to walk into this relationship and ignore that fact."

"You think it's all my fault," Kelly said, diverting her eyes. "But if you're not part of the solution, you're part of the problem."

"Whatever that means," Mom said. "The point is, I don't suffer misery gladly. Well, I did fight with my ex-husband for twenty years, but at least I had an equal shouting voice. And it wasn't misery either, just constant agitation. But in this house, I bite my tongue every day."

"Not enough," Kelly said. "Why don't you and Tristan stay out of it then? It's our business."

"It is our business when you scream at the top of your lungs at your father. It is my business when I listen to your constant judging of him. But I say nothing. It's a wonder no one has ever slapped your face."

"I'd like to see you try," Kelly said, but sounding

dry and unsteady. I could feel my own face—slapped not too long ago—burning. I wondered if anyone could see the outline of Kelly's hand on my cheek.

"Yes, I'm sure you would like to see me try."

"Mom . . . ," I said, wanting her to shut up more than I'd ever wanted her to.

"I see you treat my son like he's the one making your basketball team lose. And I say nothing. That's just not like me."

"I think you say a lot," Kelly said. "When do you ever not say something?"

"We could go to counseling, we could try to blend this family, blah, blah, blah, but, Kelly, that would be purposeless. It's not about you and me."

"I'd hate to be in one of your classes," Kelly said.

"And you won't be."

"You're just going to drop this on us, just like that?" Frank asked, a catch in his throat.

"I do not want to live my life this way."

"What have I done?" Kelly asked. "What exactly have I done?"

Mom ignored the question. "I've made a mistake, and people can correct their mistakes."

"Unless it's murder," I said under my breath.

"See, he's sarcastic, too," Kelly said.

"He's got nothing on you," Mom said. "I want peace, too, Frank. Tranquility. I don't know if that's possible in this house. I don't know if you two can work things out between yourselves, but it's sure starting to look like you can't work them out with us here."

Frank's voice came from far away. "This is so harsh."

"Frank, you and I can't talk without you getting defensive. Tristan won't talk to me about how unhappy he is here because he's afraid."

"Are you unhappy here?" Frank asked me. "Afraid of what?"

"Um . . ." I couldn't say I was afraid that there was no muzzle strong enough for my mother's mouth.

"Really, Anne," Kelly said, having recovered her calm disdain. "Aren't we being just a little melodramatic?"

"There is no *we*, Kelly," Mom retorted, and we all flinched. Then she said, "That's all I have to say. I'm not hungry anymore." She got up and took her plate to the sink. "Despite the low-calorie rabbit food."

"Well?" said Frank to no one.

"That's just like you, Anne," Kelly said. "Say what you have to say and run away."

Mom said nothing, didn't turn from the sink.

"So it's all my fault," Kelly said, sounding, for the first time since I'd known her, like that little girl I had seen at the beginning of dinner.

The room went quiet, longer this time.

"I'm sorry if that's the way it came across," Mom said, facing her, and it was almost like the two of them were connecting for a second. "Really I am. I think this is between you and your father, and we are always in the way. Tristan and I need to get out of the way."

I got up from the table, my legs pulled down by so much gravity I had to fight to move every inch. I looked at Frank's big, sad eyes, and thought that it would be something to put my hand on his shoulder and ask him to make me a sundae. But I didn't want him to think I was being sarcastic.

Chapter 16

I wasn't exactly the type to wait with gleeful antici-
pation the night before going back to school after a
break, but I had always liked school enough not to
dread it. I was usually forced to do any homework at
the beginning of the vacation long before the feared
Sunday night, so I wasn't scrambling at the last
minute. Since my parents were academics, homework was not optional in either of my houses. On
top of that, being divorced, they were both so concerned about being good parents independent of
the other that the topic of my homework came up
constantly. It was as if there were some contest
about who could be more education oriented. Still,
even though I didn't have homework hanging over
me, there was always something melancholy about
the night before school started again, like some freedom was being taken away.

This time, though, the night-before feeling was
different. I thought about how my life had changed
since even last fall. Usually on any Sunday, but especially the one right before a vacation was over, I was

at Marco's doing his homework. Tomorrow people would be talking about his party. Probably it had been huge and wild and the greatest party ever held. Also, all the fat remarks people made before Midwinter Break were making me sick about going back to that building. And Will Zumigata knew about the ceiling-busting episode.

But the worst part was that the divorce was not working out as we had planned: It was chewing at me that I had faced up to Mom about staying at Dad's. To say my mother was not an easy sell is an understatement. I had called her the morning after she had threatened to move out on Frank. She had taken the news silently at first, then kept me on the phone forever demanding words that I couldn't bring myself to say. Like a terrier digging into a foxhole, she kept at me, trying to pry a little more information out, trying to pin something definite on Kelly. At one point she was on the phone with Dad, and for a while it was like they were happily married again, screaming to hyperventilation. Maybe Kelly was their real daughter.

When Mom was back on the line with me, she demanded a live audience. I told her to pick me up and take me somewhere because I didn't want to meet at Frank's house. When she arrived at Dad's, she looked like she could kill a rabid animal with just a stare.

I got Mom out of the house and she took me to the mall where we went through the motions of shopping. Finally she spun herself out and we landed at Jagged Rock Café, which was really an all-you-can-eat sort of place with the word *café* stuck onto it. We ate in a dismal quiet for a while, until Mom stopped and actually put her face in her napkin. My mother was not a crier, and I didn't want to see her this way. Maybe she was only choking.

"Mom, what's wrong? Can you breathe, speak, or cough?"

Quickly she tossed the napkin down and threw her head back, the matter settled. "I've screwed everything up, haven't I?"

"Remember you promised? No blackmail."

"You're right. Let me rephrase that: I have screwed everything up. I jumped into this relationship with a man whose daughter I not only don't like but also actively resent, and now I've also lost my son on top of it."

"You haven't lost me. I'm still here and willing to let you buy me lunch."

"Why won't you tell me what's going on, Tri? Has she said something, done something? I need the details. What's so bad that you went running to your father?"

"Oh, come on. I didn't go running to him. Besides, I'm more of a fast-walker type of guy."

"You're avoiding the question, Tri."

"It's nothing specific," I said, trying to meet her eyes.

"That's not good enough. What is it? I want facts. Kelly being around? I know. No food or drink allowed, no TV, your staying in your room all the time to avoid her."

"Sort of. And Marco. He used to be my best friend."

"That's one good thing she did for you. That alone ought to get her into the Honor Society."

I don't know why I was still defensive of Marco. "I know you think he's a rockhead, and he is. But he was my friend, and now he doesn't even talk to me, except like I'm a pesky little brother or something."

"Well, he is the only person on Earth she gets along with," she said. "I thought Frank was going to have an aneurysm the other day talking to her. He tries so hard to stay even, keep that flat tone of voice with no emotion in it. He tries to keep control. But she won't stand for that. Oh no, she's not happy until he boils over. And then she gets on the phone with her mother to complain about him, in full earshot. Always something about his weight, as if that's the sole problem between them. But before long she's in round two, this time with Mommy. She's insatiable, that girl. If I'd wanted you to have a mean older sister, I would have borne one."

"She's just hurting," I said, mocking the therapy breath she hated. "Her inner child is fighting to get out and be loved."

"I'm going to get my own apartment, Tri. Or maybe a small house. Maybe a guillotine."

"Mom, you can't move out. Think about Frank. He's a cool guy, and Kelly will eventually go back to live with her mother."

Mom said, "But why can't you wait it out with me, then? I can set some ground rules, and if Frank won't back me up then we'll have to make other arrangements."

"She's his kid. He loves her."

"Can't he love her with a little more dignity? I don't think I've ever seen them have a moment of peace together, or a scrap of a conversation that she hasn't loaded somehow."

"Maybe—and don't get mad because I'm not saying you should go to Marco's mother—but maybe you need to see a family specialist or something."

"We need grief therapy," she said. "Because I feel like all I'm getting in this relationship is loss. The loss of the man I love, the loss of our life together, the loss of my son."

"Don't say that, Mom. I'm just saying I don't want to live there right now. You haven't lost me. I'll keep coming around. Especially when I need money."

"Oh!" she said, and put her face in her napkin again. Now I'd really done it. All I needed for this moment to be perfect was the waitress coming over and asking what Dough Boy wanted for dessert.

"Mom, I'm sorry," I said, and despite not liking this kind of thing, reached over and put my hand on hers. She lowered the napkin and her face was almost unrecognizable, like she had gotten only an hour's sleep the whole night. Her hair was a mess, but then her hair was not usually a priority.

Then her eyes relaxed and she tried to smile.

"It's just that I wanted to do things right, unlike my own parents. One kid. Not so hard to do things right with one kid. Right?" She paused and let that sink in. She had never talked to me about her parents, not in any critical way. "And I've made a complete mess."

I thought that was the end of the interview. I had told her what I needed to do and she was buying it, not without a fight, but she was buying it. I looked around for the server, wanting to get going. Mom didn't appear to be budging, though.

I said, "I want to help any way I can, except don't ask me to live there. Just for now anyway. There are other things going on. Not just Kelly. I mean, she's like the way you described her, but it's not only her. I make things more complicated being there."

"*You* don't make things more complicated. The *situation* just gets more complicated. I'm going to have to think about this, Tri, though my inclination is to leave."

"Promise me you won't do anything right away. I don't want to make things harder for Frank either. He's a good guy."

"You're not the one making it hard for him."

"I know, but if you leave and then Kelly goes back to her mother's again, he'll be all alone."

She grabbed my hands this time. "It's very gratifying for me that you like Frank. A mother always worries."

"Well, he's a good cook, for one thing."

"You're a good kid, you know that?"

"Yes."

"I intend to take full credit for you."

"Will you say that someday when I'm on trial?"

"Maybe." She looked at the salad bar. "Let's get some pudding."

"Kelly wouldn't approve."

Her eyes widened. "No, she wouldn't."

"Good. Get some for both of us."

So that's how we discussed what I didn't want to discuss, and how I got around Mom, for the time being. But Sunday night as I lay in my bed with my obstinate friend Dread, he had to scuffle with Guilt in the fight to keep me awake. I felt like I had abandoned Mom, and although Frank was not my father and I hadn't known him too long, it was as if I had dumped him altogether. And even though Kelly didn't want me at her house, my absence might make her angry. She might exact some further revenge on me at school, as if telling people about the attic floor breaking underneath me wasn't enough. I wanted to bypass Monday morning like nothing else. What other place could I get enrolled in before 7:30 A.M.? There had to be a school where the people were big, and a round kid would be respected. Maybe Samoa.

There was one other thing in my crazy head that night that I couldn't figure out, but it felt like a positive mystery. Usually I tried to go on a diet a couple days before a school vacation was coming to an end, in case I gained some weight while sitting around at home, or even if I hadn't, to look like I was getting skinny. I hadn't tried a last-minute diet this time. The thought hadn't even occurred to me. I had gone cross-country skiing or snowshoeing every day of the vacation, either with Dad and Cyndi or Peter or alone. I hadn't lost any weight that I could tell, even though I didn't get on the scale because Cyndi had banished them from the house. But I felt different in some way that I couldn't explain. And, unlike the usual ways that I felt different from kids my age, this gave me a feeling of accelerating into something good. I just didn't know exactly where I was going.

Chapter 17

The next morning I tried to keep up with a crowd of people as I hurried into the school. I had made it all the way on the bus and into the building and not yet had I heard a nasty remark. No fat talk, nothing about breaking the floor. Maybe a new world order had been born. In homeroom no one was particularly interested in me. Then Mr. Matthews got on the horn, and the morning announcements were underway. He went through his usual list of things that, though predictably boring, were difficult to ignore because of the volume. Then he launched into an unspirited lecture about respect that I never would have seen coming if I'd had a telescopic crystal ball:

"Remember, ladies and gentlemen, we have rules of conduct in this building, and if that's not good enough for you, we have laws to back them up. You might think that pushing and shoving and name calling is fun for you, and that it entertains your friends, but you are wrong. Harassment is a crime and will be prosecuted. Green Hills High School does not discriminate on the basis of race, creed, color, ethnic origin . . . "

He paused, took a deep breath, and let it out, as

if trying to remember what else was on that shopping list. *"Gender. Or handicap. Age. Physical appearance. Or sexual orientation."*

He waited a few seconds, but apparently he couldn't remember any more groups Green Hills didn't discriminate against. *"I expect you to uphold that policy, or you will suffer the consequences. You think the kid in gym class isn't masculine enough? You keep it to yourself. You don't like the color of someone's skin? Too bad for you. You think it's funny to pick on the kid who's got a little spare tire around his waist? It's not. I will personally investigate any complaints of harassment."*

I shook my head like, What a dope this guy is, as if I couldn't possibly fall into one of those categories.

Now his enthusiasm was starting to falter.

"Please report, uh, to me, any complaints. And I will . . . and I will handle them."

Then, like his battery pack had a surge, he bounced back:

"Students are parking their cars haphazardly around the parking lot. There are a limited number of spaces in the student lot, and if that's full, you may not use the faculty parking lot. So DO NOT PARK BEYOND THE YELLA LINES! As of tomorrow, students who PARK BEYOND THE

YELLA LINES *will be subject to a* PARKING FINE. *Your grades and transcripts to colleges will not be released if these fines are not paid.*"

Breathing heavy now that he had finished the race, he tried to speak more sedately, *"Today's menu is . . ."*

The day had started with a glimmer that maybe all my apprehensions were a waste of time. But here was the most boring person who'd ever lived telling everybody they weren't supposed to pick on the fat boy. Who had told him? Had he just picked up on it himself, being more intuitive than he appeared? Or was he just getting his ethics duty over with so he could get on with important things like parking justice? I labeled him a traitor and scheduled a meeting with him in the Tower of London. This time I wouldn't miss.

Just as I was thinking that I would not be able to move from my seat ever again, that the maintenance men would have to come and remove me, Mr. Matthews came back on the intercom for one more announcement:

"Excuse me, please. Students interested in signing up for the cross-country skiing club should see Mrs. Magruder in room 213 during activity period tomorrow. This is a

noncompetitive sport for those interested in learning how to de-
velop their cross-country skiing skills."

A kernel of optimism sprouted inside me. Maybe I would go sign up.

While I had never been fond of lunchtime at the high school, now I especially dreaded it. I could skip lunch, which would mean avoiding all the hazards but going hungry and weak. Or I could take the plunge and talk nonstop while I got my food down fast enough to keep from seeing or hearing things around me. It was like not having any hot water in your house and having to decide if you went out in the world smelly or jumped into a cold shower and got frosty clean. The best thing to do was not be late, but this rushing to the cafeteria was risky because it could be construed as the fat boy wanting to get there first. It was a chance I usually had to take.

Instead, that day I found myself in the worst possible lunchtime position. I had been bringing my lunch to avoid the long lines and bad food, but that morning I was running late for the bus. There was some money in my backpack, which was one good thing; but I stayed too long cleaning up after a bio lab, and by the time I got washed up and threw my books in my locker, the line was out the cafeteria door and down the hall. I had to stand at the end of it. I didn't know anyone either, not enough to talk to, so I couldn't make conversation to block out any remarks in the wind. The line moved like a listless snail; a couple times I almost bolted. The authorities didn't care if you skipped lunch, just if you skipped classes. But it would mean going without food, and I was growling hollow inside. Or I could come back when the line was shorter, but by then the cafeteria would be full and I might not find a seat, especially if Peter and the gang didn't think I was coming and didn't save me one. I would have to walk by all those tables full of people, looking for a home.

All this planning and replanning passed the time, and I finally got my lunch, a bare-bones meal. In an attempt to be health conscious (or to save the government-surplus meat for harder times) the cafeteria had started serving a vegetarian entrée every day. Today's was especially creative, a plate of steamed vegetables with a side of glue-factory-by-product rice. Still, it was food for the time being. There was always Dad's house (with its cupboards influenced by Cyndi) waiting for me after school.

With this yummy meal on my tray, I paid the cashier and turned toward the open sea of people. I felt weak for a second, like I couldn't take another step forward. Then I saw Peter waving to me from the very farthest corner. Why couldn't he sit closer for once? Oh, well, at least it looked like I was home free. He was sitting with Anthony and Gretchen as usual, and I looked forward to seeing them, if not to eating lunch itself. But halfway to my seat there was one huge table I would have to either go right past or go far out of my way not to go by. That would look really obvious. Even trying not to, I saw that the table was full of some of the most evil people on the planet—Marco, Kelly, Will Zumigata, and Heather Baird, the girl who Marco had taken on his boat before he and Kelly discovered snow sex. I held hard on to my tray, looking toward my friends and smiling like I wasn't walking past unfed lions. I braced myself for something bad, a sound effect of an explosion, for example, or at least some nasty snickering.

Just as I was chastising myself for once again being a big baby, thinking I was so important that everyone was always planning on tormenting me, I heard someone much like Will Zumigata say, "Don't trip." Then something caught hard on my feet and I went hurtling forward.

A nightmare played out by day. In the sickening cascade of falling, I didn't try to save my tray or keep myself upright. There was a clang and drop, and I was on the floor. For a few chronic seconds I tried to get up, moving mechanically, still startled. I gathered broccoli and carrots and cauliflower and muddy rice onto my upside-down tray.

And I still had this dumb smile. Even when the world had spilled all over me, I wanted to make sure people didn't think I was a poor sport. I might have hated the smile more than Will Zumigata at that moment, the sewn-on smile I wore even though venom pulsed through me and I wanted to shove my tray wide side down his throat.

It almost scared me, what surging hatred felt like. But that hatred was not just about him. It was the frustration of undeniable, absolute failure. He had exposed me. I had tried to hide, for almost two years, always looking over my shoulder, wearing baggy clothes, deflecting comments, trying not to be caught in the halls alone, taking the easy gym mod, eating food I didn't want. And it had amounted to nothing. One wrong step and I was sticking out of someone's bedroom ceiling. One stupid little practical joke and there my tubby body was, in the center of the floor, covered with food, in front of everyone. The laughing, like a chorus of maniacs, made my head vibrate. On the floor, astounded and wet and dizzy, I thought just for a second it might be best to lie down and fake death. Anything would be better than looking in the face of that laughter. Someone said, "At least the floor didn't break."

When the good cheer began to die down, there was another commotion.

"Did you trip him?"

It was Mr. Matthews's voice. Now there was no doubt that he could get angry over something besides disorderly parking. I finally got on my feet as Mr. Matthews held his makeshift trial.

"Answer me, Mr. Zumigata."

"No," he wailed, guilty enough.

"Why are all your friends congratulating you, then? Mr. Cavi seems to have enjoyed your performance immensely."

"I don't know." Will looked a lot smaller now, sitting next to Mr. Matthews's tower of a body.

Then there was another familiar voice, low but forceful. "You tripped him?"

"I didn't do it. He just fell."

"Did somebody trip you?" Mr. Matthews asked me as harshly as he had Will. "Or did you slip?"

I tried to stand up straight. "I don't know," I said, my throat full of lint.

"Yes or no? Did someone trip you?"

"I don't know."

"You idiot," Kelly said. Then, as if this lunch period could get any more unbelievable, she smacked Will's face so hard his glasses flew across the table. She didn't stop there. Like she was an expert at this kind of thing, she tipped the stuff off her lunch tray, picked it up, and brought it down toward his head. Before this knighting could happen, Mr. Matthews grabbed the tray and had control.

"That's enough!" he demanded, loud and final, silencing the room. Then he took Will Zumigata away from the table by the arm, still carrying Kelly's tray with his other hand.

"Get to my office. Now! Before any other girls deck you." There was only a trickle of laughter because a new Mr. Matthews was in town.

"And you," he said, pointing the tray at Kelly, "keep your hands to yourself. Clean this mess up before you find yourself suspended, too." People were gathering around to help clean me up, so I didn't see Kelly approach until she was in front of me. I flinched when she raised her hand to me, thinking I was next on her list of guys to slam. Instead, she picked food off me, straightened the collar on my shirt.

"You're always getting into messes, like a little boy," she said. "Like a little brother."

I could see Marco still sitting at his table. He looked around, probably to see if there were cue cards telling him what to do now, then sheepishly got up and walked out of the cafeteria.

"Are you okay?" Kelly asked.

"Yeah, I guess."

She gave me a businesslike smile, then turned and left, presumably after Marco. Someone dabbed at me with napkins, and a bunch of people were mopping up the floor, Peter and Gretchen and Anthony and a couple of cafeteria women. Oh, and Tara Montoya. Tara Montoya was brushing food off my chest with her hand. It was the closest I'd ever come to having a date. Maybe I would try to buy her a car or something in exchange for her kindness, cosign a loan at least. People kept buzzing around me trying to help. They were insistent to the point where I was even getting a little annoyed, except with Tara Montoya who could buzz until she dropped.

"Better?" she asked. But it didn't matter what she said. It all sounded like beauty in the darkness.

"Yeah," I said a little hoarsely. "Thanks." She touched my arm and went back to her seat. It's amazing how humiliation and rapture could share the same space inside me.

When I was finally sitting in a seat instead of crawling on the floor, one of the cafeteria ladies brought me another plate of vegetarian muck, which I tried to be grateful for.

"What a jerk Zumigata is," Gretchen said. "So seventh grade."

"Let's talk about something else," I said.

"Right," she said. "Let's discuss these brownies my mother made." She pulled out a foil square and opened it. "Triple layer. Her specialty." Peter and Anthony both reached for them. I made an attempt to eat something on my glue plate. But Gretchen persisted. "Tristan, you need a brownie after all that. Take one."

I hesitated, then smiled at her. "Okay," I said, and lifted a dense block of chocolate off the foil. It was the best thing I had eaten in school in years.

I made up my mind then and there to join the cross-country club. I wasn't skinny and fast but neither is a mule, and he has his purpose. Maybe underneath my thin skin, a thicker one would grow.

Chapter 18

Mom was waiting for me at Dad's when I got there that night. This was more bad news. Either someone had died, or she had finally discovered that I was the one who had eaten her Godiva chocolates last Easter. She was waiting in the driveway, looking grim. Her hair looked worse, if possible.

"Mom, what's wrong? You're not supposed to be here. Did someone die?"

"No. No one's dead."

"Good." Relief unsnapped through my body. Then I remembered she might leave Frank. "Did you run away from home?"

"It was either be here or at Frank's trying not to kill Kelly."

"What'd she do this time?"

"I got this today. An e-mail from Marco's mother. The therapist." She handed me a sheet of paper with words in tiny print on a quarter of the page:

Dear Anne—I just want you to know that you can call me ANY TIME about Tristan. Just tell my secretary it's you and I'll make space. I also want you to know that Marco had nothing to do with tripping Tristan in the cafeteria, as Mr. Matthews has charged. I know Marco and Tristan do not spend much time together anymore. That's just the way it is with kids growing up, but he would never, ever do anything to hurt Tristan. Of course, Dr. Cavi and I have contacted our attorney about this false accusation, so we assume Marco will be fully exonerated shortly.

I also want you to know that Tristan can talk to me ANY TIME he wants—free of charge, and I mean that. Many children have issues with their weight at this age, and I know it's hard when a kid has to deal with being teased. Remember it's not what you're eating that's the problem, it's what's eating you! Again, please call just as soon as you get a chance. Remember, you're only as sick as your secrets!

Angela Fiero, M.S.W.

I wondered if I would ever again be surprised by anything. I gave it back to her.

"I want to know what's going on and I want to know now. The idea that this . . . this amateur knows something about my own son that I don't makes me . . ." She sucked in a harsh breath. "Makes me want to get in touch with some real rage."

My insides were almost completely frozen. "I don't know——"

"Don't give me that crap, Tri. I know when you're trying to wriggle out of something, and I always let it go because you're growing up and I don't want you to think I'm as meddling as I am. But this! This is going to drive me around the bend. Now tell me."

"Mom, I don't want to do this," I said. "It's my life."

Dad drove up next. "My God, what's wrong?" he asked, jumping out of the SUV. "Someone's died?"

"No one is dead!" Mom said.

"Well, then what is it?"

She thrust the e-mail into his hands. He read it, looked up at me confused.

"Let's go inside," he said.

Once in the living room I made one last attempt to be something more than a child. "I don't want to do this," I said.

"Tristan," my father said with an authority he seldom used with me, "I want to know what Marco's mother is talking about."

"I want to know now," my mother butted in.

"Give him a second, Anne," Dad said. Then he continued with me in a nicer tone like he had a split personality. "You can tell us anything, Tri. I mean it. You will get absolutely nothing but support from us."

"I know," I said.

"Then what is it? What's this about getting tripped in the cafeteria? This isn't kindergarten, for God's sake."

I fished around in my head for some smart-ass reply, for some lie even, but it was all too much. I knew my face was steaming red anyway, and this probing so near to my soul made me collapse. I sat down and started to bawl.

The wailing was addictively soothing, like digging your fingernails into an itch. I cried and cried, and the intensity kept building, not dropping. The addiction stabbed at me until I was crossing over into some kind of spastic fit. No one tried to touch me as I convulsed.

I'm not sure how long it took for the heaving in

my chest to settle to heavy breathing. By then my wet face was completely covered with sweat, snot, and tears.

"I just want to say," I started tremulously, "that other kids handle their own problems."

"Like Marco?" Dad challenged. "He handles his own problems?" After I mopped up some, he continued, very gently. "Do you really think he's capable of handling his own problems? His parents have to call in a lawyer every time he misses the bus."

"Do you really think, Dad," I said in my quavering voice, "that Marco ever took a school bus?"

"Then look at Kelly," Mom said. "With her trim body and her big fat attitude. I think the long-distance operator is her only friend sometimes. No, Tri, other kids—normal kids—need someone. So what's going on at school that's so horrible you can't tell your old mother?"

"Would you have told *your* old mother?" I asked, not looking at her.

"Well, no," she said, not missing a beat. "But there was no point in telling my old mother anything."

"The only way we can help," Dad said, "is if we know everything."

So I told them the whole story—well, a good chunk of it minus the sex. There was no holding back. Once you start confessing, you just want to be completely cleansed. I told them about how I didn't like school anymore because I was afraid all the time. I told them that it wasn't just about Kelly and Marco, but they had made things worse, making fun of my stupid Christmas candles, getting caught at Marco's, and slapping me in various ways.

"And by the way, Mom. If you ever go into Kelly's room—if the security alarm doesn't go off—you'll see an interesting pattern in her ceiling. I did that. I fell through the damn ceiling, halfway anyway. And I also landed on the cafeteria floor. I'm always falling. That's the way it is for me."

"What other stuff happened at school?" Dad asked. "What else did they do to you?"

I told them about Will Zumigata and the kids on the ledge and Tim Boggs and how either Marco or Kelly or both had repeated the ceiling story and now people were laughing about it. I concluded with, "That's all the truth you said you wanted."

They waited, like there was more truth. Then Dad said, "Well, do they not like you for some reason? Did you get in some fight or something with somebody?"

"It's because I'm alive," I said.

"But I don't get it," Dad said. "Why wouldn't they like you?"

"I don't know," I said.

"What is it, Tri?"

I looked at him, wondering when he had gone deaf. "Nothing," I said, giving up. They just weren't going to get it. "Everything's fine."

We all waited while my lie died in the air.

"What else is there?" Mom asked. "The whole truth, and quickly. I'm starting to dream up ways to package Kelly to send back to her mother. I'm thinking duct tape."

"I'm a little heavy," I said.

"That's not a good reason," said Mom.

"They don't need a better reason," I said.

Dad looked at Mom with that familiar dead look. "There's your mother to consider. If she hadn't gone and gotten involved with that doormat boyfriend of hers, at least you wouldn't have to deal with Miss Body Fat Index."

"Dad," I said, before Mom could retaliate.

"It's not my fault, Gordon," she said, "although that's very convenient for you."

"Shut up, Anne."

"How clever, Gordon. Did you stay up all night thinking that one up?"

"I stay up a lot of nights worrying about my son. Try it sometime."

"I do worry about him. Don't sit there on your throne and tell me I'm not worrying about my son."

They kept arguing, not noticing me. They were truly asking for it. Begging, really.

Finally I stood up, took a deep breath, and shouted at the top of my unchanged voice, *"Will you two shut the hell up?"*

Having a high voice had its benefits because they did in fact shut the hell up. They both gaped at me like they were brain damaged.

"What do you think it is?" I asked. "I'm fat. Nobody hates me, they just want to have a little fun, that's all. That's all. Why can't you two understand that? Why do you keep asking me questions and not listening? Just both of you shut up." I stood there a moment in case there were any more eruptions still in my lungs. Then I dropped into my seat, waited.

Mom whispered, "You know I don't like that expression. 'Shut up.'"

I looked at her, not quite believing what she'd said. Then the absurdity hit, and as if the tension in me had really only been bottled-up laughter, I burst. I laughed so hard I could barely breathe.

When I was done, even though I ached from laughing, I felt lighter than I had since starting high school. I looked at them and said, "I'm going to be okay."

"That's obvious," Mom said.

"Mom," I warned. "Listen to me."

"Okay. Okay. I just don't know what exactly to do," she said, "but I'm not going to have my son harassed in school—"

"It's okay. It helps talking to you both. It really does. As long as you aren't talking at the same time."

"Well . . . can I at least compose an answer to M.S.W. Fiero explaining that we do not need her help?"

"No, leave it. Just leave it."

"Your father can help me."

"Are you in the same room as me? I said no."

"Are you positive there's nothing we can do for you?" Dad asked. "Anything?"

"You have," I said. "Just be around. But don't always do the talking. And shut up about each other. Oh, sorry, Mom. I mean, be quiet about each other."

"Tri . . ."

"I mean it," I said. "Leave it at that."

They danced around me a little more, making sure that what I wanted wasn't what they thought I should want. They didn't look completely convinced or satisfied, but I was going to let that be their problem.

Mom eventually got ready to leave. "Well, I guess then it's good-bye, everyone. It's been a great deal of fun. I'm now going home to face some music I've been ignoring for too long now." She kissed me. I felt I ought to tell them one more fact before she went home to Kelly and Frank.

"Wait. This is kind of weird, but when Will Zumigata tripped me, Kelly smacked him 'cross the face."

"Is that her trademark? Slapping faces?" Dad gave an irritated wave as if he were completely sick of Kelly. Mom said, "That doesn't excuse much about her."

"Yeah, but then she almost broke his skull with a tray afterward. Which would have been kind of cool, in a way."

Mom frowned. "That doesn't give her a great deal of credibility with me."

I thought of how Kelly had done some other violence for me, thrown a rock at the truck. I considered giving them that one more piece of evidence. Then I changed my mind.

"Well, I'm just saying, listen or don't, as you always say."

"We'll see," said Mom.

"Good-bye, Anne," my father said.

"See ya," Mom said. "Wish me luck. I think I might actually enjoy living in the Motel 8 for a while."

Mom did call the next day to say she was staying at a motel near the interstate.

"Frank and I had it out last night, Tri," she said, somewhat apologetically.

"Mom . . ."

"I know, I know. I tried to be calm, I tried to be rational, but when I got home and Kelly was not there, but was at Marco's house, that pretty well did it. Boom! Through the roof."

"Why do you care if she's at Marco's?"

"I don't know. I don't really. It's just the privilege. The constant privilege."

"What did Frank say?"

"He was slightly curious about the ceiling you fell through, for one. But mainly he was defensive of her."

"Well, yeah."

"Yes, but he couldn't even accept the possibility that she is brutal. I went on and on, and once again it came back to me that this was really about him and his daughter, and we had gotten in the middle of it. You for sure were a target. So I told him that I didn't see any other way around it. I had to leave and he had to make peace with his daughter."

"Was he upset?"

There was dumb silence. "What do you think?"

"Yeah, okay."

"So I packed what I could, and just as he was helping me put a few bags into the car, who should waltz in but the royal couple."

"What happened then?" I asked, fearing all possible scenarios.

"Not much. Kelly used her haughty air with me. I was a little sarcastic with Marco. Oh, well," she said, "so Frank and I are on trial separation, which is what married couples call it, which is what we didn't want to be. Like I said, nothing has turned out the way I planned."

"Sorry, Ma."

"No, it's up to me. Leave it to me. I'll make things right. Oh, by the way, I made Frank go up to the attic with me to examine those holes you made. He's going to have a carpenter finish the entire floor. Marco said he would help. Frank said no thanks. I don't think Marco could pick out a floor plank in a police line-up."

Chapter 19

Mrs. Magruder was standing at the front of her health classroom, a pile of notebooks and textbooks, a backpack, and what looked like an old lunch all balanced precariously on her desk. Pulled down in front of her blackboard was a huge map featuring a faceless naked man and woman back-to-back, the internals of their genitalia diagramed. There were posters everywhere, about the heart, about STDs, about drugs and hugs. Stacks of paper cluttered every surface.

I didn't have her for a class, but I had seen her hustling through the building; everybody had because she was a human landmark. She didn't look frazzled or unkempt or ditsy, just overly ambitious. She was always holding a million objects, as if it were the most natural thing to walk down the halls carrying six copies of *Our Bodies, Ourselves* and hiking gear for a three-month trip. She was a safe teacher, though, a lovable mess, one of those buoyant and forgiving people who probably liked everyone.

"First, this is noncompetitive," she tried to shout,

but her voice was cloned from Minnie Mouse. "I re-
peat, noncompetitive. We will not be having meets
with other schools; we will not be having tryouts,
and you will not earn a varsity letter for this sport.
This is an extracurricular activity for those of you
who would like to learn how to ski or improve your
skiing, and get some cheap exercise. What we do
have is discounts for the trails at Hatfield Country
Club, which, as you may know, has the best trails in
the area. And we do have a bus to take us there
every Tuesday and Thursday after school. Again,
this is a club, not a sport. Well, okay, it's a sport, but
not a competition.

"You must bring your own equipment and you
must wear proper and appropriate clothing." She
emphasized the *must* to sound authoritative, but you
could tell she was trying too hard. "I will not allow
anyone on the bus who is underdressed, especially in
very cold weather." She paused. "And that brings me
to another point," she said as if she hadn't just
thought of it. "We will not ski if it's excessively cold.
I'll make the determination that day by morning announcements. If you have trouble attaining equipment, see me and we'll try to work something out."

I could picture her "attaining" skis for a needy

kid by buying them new with her own money, then claiming she had found them in her cellar.

The first actual ski trip was Thursday after school, three more days I had made it through since my annihilation in the cafeteria. There had been two more incidents in those three days. Two goofy red-headed twins who were freshmen and looked like a science experiment had called me a sumo wrestler as they gawked at me. I almost laughed in their identical faces because they looked so weird and so curious. Tim Boggs had said, "Hey, Slim" as he walked by in a marijuana-induced haze. I considered a nasty and profane and very clever retort, but it wouldn't have helped. Unless you had a magic wand—or a slingshot—there was no good way to defend yourself or prevent future assaults. Maybe these strikes just happened in random bunches. Anyway, I was three days closer to the end of the school year and the summer heat might kill off the fungus.

This was my first ever high-school club, my first ever high-school sport. Mrs. Magruder showed up late like you would expect her to, looking something like a Christmas tree in the fourth dimension. She was balancing skis, poles, three sweaters, her boots, a cloth bag full of papers, and an enormous open pocketbook with her wallet teetering at the top of the pile. Again she tried to sound bossy as she took attendance and went over the rules. Peter was there and Gretchen, too. Anthony wouldn't come because he was afraid of hills.

And someone else was there who never failed to capture my attention: Tara Montoya, the girl of my dreams—and believe me I knew I was dreaming. She had on winter clothes that looked smart on her, a heavy knit white sweater with a tiny rose embroidered near her right shoulder, and black spandex ski pants. She didn't look fiercely fashionable like Kelly would have, just comfortable and nice. And the best part? She was totally uncoordinated on her skis, as limp as a loose bungee cord. I loved how she asked for help, and I loved how we had to wait for her. I loved pretending to be impatient and having to help her get back up when she fell like a sunbeam on the snow time after time. I loved the way she asked us not to go too fast, "especially you, Tristan. You're like a bullet." I was finally an expert at something, or sort of an expert, and it was a million times more gratifying than being the brain who did Marco's homework. There were no strings with her, no secret agreement about why I had to be helpful. Although she would never be my girlfriend, she might someday be a friend of mine. I pretended I wasn't as good at skiing as I was, and didn't make any attempt to show off because I would wind up in a snowbank if I did. The universe always punished arrogance, at least mine.

I wondered how life could be both nasty and sweet. While Peter and I were being heroes to Tara Montoya, I thought I could live my whole life in these moments. There was nothing I wanted more than just being with her and my friends.

There were wild animals waiting for me, but they couldn't get through this bubble, not right now. At times I even forgot that life could be hell because now there was a perfection to it that couldn't coexist with the world of fat and ugly remarks and parties I wasn't invited to.

The next night I got a call I wasn't expecting.

"Tristan, it's Frank."

"Hi," I said, trying not to sound guilty.

"Can you come over? Kelly has something to say to you."

I had some idea what this was about and I didn't like it at all, but I wasn't feeling sharp enough to find a way out.

"Um, I have a lot of homework."

"It's Friday, Tristan. Please. It's important."

So I called Mom who drove me over to Frank's. She came in with me.

"I won't listen if you don't want me to," she said, "but I will pack a few more things while I wait."

"No," Kelly said with her usual supremacy. "You need to hear this, too, although you probably won't believe me."

To be honest, I couldn't believe any of this was happening, especially not that I was sitting down to the second powwow that centered on me in the course of a week.

"Tristan," Kelly said, sitting close enough that her perfume began to engulf me. "I broke up with Marco last night."

"Oh. Sorry." I really was surprised by this, but I couldn't figure out why she would call me over here on a Friday night to tell me of all people. So all I could muster up was another, "Oh."

"I want to tell you from the bottom of my heart that I never said anything to anyone about the ceiling incident. No one." My face flashed red. I wondered if Frank was going to demand money for repairs.

"Okay."

"You don't believe me, I know. But it's true. Marco is a child. I've learned that. He betrayed me by going out with another girl." She didn't say who. I prayed it wasn't Tara Montoya. "I'm used to betrayal," she said, and looked over at her father who rolled his eyes, but sadly.

Then, because I had to say something, I blurted, "How was Marco's party?"

"Great," she said. "He got drunk and he slept with Melissa Furman after I left."

"Oh."

"Everybody knew but me."

"I'm sorry," I said.

"Oh, well, she's got big thighs," she said. "I guess that's what he likes. Anyway I told you a long time ago I know what it's like to be heavy, and I would never do anything to make it harder for you." Out of the corner of my eye I saw Mom start as if she were going to meddle, but I gave her a warning look.

"It's true. And as for Marco, he's just a boy. That's the problem. He was the only person that I really loved. I thought I loved him anyway."

She drew a long, meaningful sigh. Then her brow wrinkled, as if she were just now understanding something. "We have that much in common. We were both fooled by Marco. I should have stuck to our walking schedule instead of getting involved with him. You know, Tri," she said, using the name only my family used, "sometimes I think it's easier for people to be bad to each other than to be good. Just easier. I guess it comes naturally. Being kind is work."

She looked away. "Little brother. I always wanted one. Or a sister. My parents were too selfish, though."

Then she grew distant, dismissive. "Anyway that's what I had to say."

"Yeah, okay," I said. I didn't know how to behave when someone who was not often very nice to me was nice to me. Then some words came tumbling out on their own. "Do you want to go cross-country skiing with me sometime? I'm getting faster."

She looked at me as if it had been meant as an insult. But that's not how I'd meant it and she must have seen my expression because she said, "I think that would be fun. Maybe we can. I'm probably moving back to Buffalo, though. But maybe. Before I go."

Kelly turned to Mom. "I know you blame me for you breaking up with Dad."

"No," Mom started to say, "it's not that simple—"

"It never is with you, Anne," Kelly said, and I was almost relieved she had cut Mom off before we had to hear her interpretation again. "Let me finish. I'm sorry, that's all. That's not what I wanted to happen."

Mom looked like she was going to argue but then stopped herself. There was a first time for everything. "Okay," was all she said.

"Okay," Kelly said. "Maybe someday just think about it from my side." Before my mother could say anything else, Kelly ended the conversation. "Well, good night."

"Night," I said, but I sat there, not comprehending that it was really time to go. I was looking at Kelly, realizing that popularity is something assigned by people who think they're not popular. I had given her royalty status without even thinking, and yet it was Friday night and she was home without a boyfriend, without any friends around. I thought of my own friends, Gretchen and Peter and Anthony, and how I had taken them lightly to follow Marco.

"Good night, Tristan," she said more stiffly.

"Oh yeah, good night," I said.

When I was near the back door, Frank surprised me by grabbing my arms and giving me a hug that he held too long. I didn't try to pull away before he was ready.

He held me away from him, his hands on my shoulders. For a moment he looked me in the eyes. I used all the effort I had to keep from looking away.

"I just want you to know two things," he said. "First, I only weigh 290 pounds, no matter what my daughter might have told you. She always rounds up."

I laughed.

"And the other thing is that I'm glad I wasn't with you in the attic. Or we'd both be embedded in the cellar floor right now."

He hugged me again, rubbing my head.

"So long," he said when he finally let me go. Thankfully he didn't say "I love you" or something awful like that, but I had a rock in my throat anyway.

"Bye, Frank."

He cupped my chin. I smiled, but it made me want to cry and I was so sick of tears. I turned around to go.

Mom and I drove in silence to Dad's house. For some reason I was irritated with her. I got to wondering what Kelly had meant about seeing it from her side. Mom was a great mother, but my stomach turned thinking about what it must be like to have her as a stepmother. *Great* probably wasn't the word. *Grate*, maybe.

Mom may have sensed my agitation, because she didn't say anything until we got to Dad's house. By then the anger had passed. "Sure you don't want to spend the night in the motel with me? Clean bathroom? Cable? All the ice you can eat?"

"Thanks anyway, Mom." I kissed her good-bye then stole into Dad's house. My whole body felt foreign, charged, like I would start vibrating at any second. It wasn't necessarily an unpleasant sensation, but it was like I was standing half out of myself.

When I was in bed and couldn't sleep for the stew of mysteries inside me, I put on some clothes and snuck out of the house with my skis and headed for the elementary-school field. Within minutes I could feel my heart pounding in a good way, the sweat breaking out, and the worry and fear dripping away into the snow I planed.

There was going to be more grief at school—any school—maybe until the day I graduated. Maybe instead of my name they'd call me Dough

Boy when I went up for my diploma, or maybe somebody would trip me as I walked to the stage. I couldn't control it if they did. But I was ready for them all now, with a little dread, but not the kind that controls your every breath. If there were fragile bones inside even the prettiest, thinnest, and most popular body, maybe appearance was just politics.

It was very quiet, almost eerie, and there was no one I could call out to here if I needed to. But the moon was big—full and fat and in command—and I thought of how Mom and Dad would hate that I was out alone so late at night. I glided on and on, almost unafraid.